A SCANDALOUS SECRET

SPIES AND LOVERS

LAURA TRENTHAM

*A*s the daughter of England's spymaster, Miss Victoria Hawkins is no stranger to secrets. Her biggest secret is the tender feelings she holds for Thomas Garrick, her father's personal guard. As the pressure to choose a husband at an upcoming Christmas house party mounts, Victoria grows desperate. When circumstances trap them together in a cottage with a single bed and a bottle of brandy, her infatuation with the gruff Garrick might cause the scandal of the season...and give Victoria exactly what she wishes for this Christmas.

ALSO BY LAURA TRENTHAM

Historical Romance
Spies and Lovers

An Indecent Invitation Book 1
A Brazen Bargain, Book 2
A Reckless Redemption, Book 3
A Sinful Surrender, Book 4
A Wicked Wedding, Book 5
A Daring Deception, Book 6
A Scandalous Secret, Book 7
Spies and Lovers Boxset

CONTEMPORARY ROMANCE
Sweet Home Alabama Novels

Slow and Steady Rush, Book 1
Caught Up in the Touch, Book 2
Melting Into You, Book 3
Christmas in the Cop Car, Novella 3.5
The Sweet Home Alabama Collection

. . .

HIGHLAND, Georgia Novels
A Highlander Walks Into a Bar, Book 1
A Highlander in a Pickup, Book 2
A Highlander is Coming to Town, Book 3

HEART OF A HERO Novels
The Military Wife
An Everyday Hero

COTTONBLOOM NOVELS
Kiss Me That Way, Book 1
Then He Kissed Me, Book 2
Till I Kissed You, Book 3

CHRISTMAS IN THE COP CAR, Novella 3.5
Light Up the Night, Novella 3.75

LEAVE THE NIGHT ON, Book 4
When the Stars Come Out, Book 5
Set the Night on Fire, Book 6

FIELDSTONES ADVENTURE NOVELLAS by Leah Trent
An Impetuous Interlude, Fieldstones Adventure Book 1
A Naughty Notion, Fieldstones Adventure Book 2
A Mysterious Masquerade, Fieldstones Adventure Book 3
A Dangerous Desire, Fieldstones Adventure Book 4
The Fieldstones Adventures Boxset

I love to hear from readers! Come find me:

Laura@LauraTrentham.com

www.LauraTrentham.com

Sign up for Laura's Newsletter

Join Laura's Facebook Squad

Are you interested in receiving a FREE book?!

Join my newsletter! There will be links in your Welcome Email for TWO free books!

Sign up for Laura's Newsletter

CHAPTER 1

$\mathcal{T}$homas Garrick stood sentinel outside Sir Hawkins's study. His stance was deliberately casual, but he remained on alert at all times, even in the London town house Sir Hawkins and his family called home. He didn't try to be intimidating, yet the young scullery maid gave him a wide berth on her daily chores. He'd made the mistake of smiling at her once. She'd acted like he was planning to gobble her up and spit out her bones.

He was often stationed outside Sir Hawkins's study in case he was needed to confer on operations, deliver sensitive messages, escort Sir Hawkins to and from Westminster, or less often these days, safeguard Lady Hawkins or Miss Hawkins on their errands. Garrick was the only man Hawkins trusted with his family, life, and secrets.

The Hawkins's only child, Victoria, traipsed down the stairs in a long-sleeved frock of buttercup yellow, glowing like she had swallowed the sun on the chilly winter day. Her unruly black hair had been braided and pinned up, but sprigs had escaped to curl around her temple and nape. Her complexion was rosy and betrayed her forays into the garden without her bonnet even as the weather had turned colder.

Watching her from under his lashes, Garrick remained perfectly still so he could study her unawares for as long as possible. A pensive expression had settled on her features, but it was not truly at home there. Victoria's disposition was usually as sunny and optimistic as her frock. What was she considering with such focus that she still hadn't spotted him only an arm's length away as she took the last step?

"Good morn, Miss Hawkins," he said formally.

She jerked away from him as if she expected an attack, her hand at her throat. He straightened and touched her elbow, surprised at the vehemence of her reaction. She grasped his forearm and moved closer to him. It was his turn to stifle surprise.

The touch was intimate, and she didn't let go, not even when their gazes clashed. He found it impossible to plumb the depths of her dark blue eyes for her thoughts. She had been a mystery to him since the day Sir Hawkins had brought him into his home like a stray puppy. His interactions with the opposite sex had been nonexistent at the orphanage, and memories of his time before tragedy befell him had faded.

Since reaching manhood, his experience had broadened, of course, but she was still more fascinating and complicated than any woman of his acquaintance. Her nature was in turns bubbly and introspective. The superficial facade she presented to her callers was often undercut by wry observations that reminded him of her father, whose intellect and logic made him a formidable weapon as England's spymaster.

Only inches separated them. For his own sanity, he'd done his best to keep his distance the past two years. She was a lady whose mother expected her to marry into the ton to broaden and expand the family's connections. The orphaned son of a blacksmith did not qualify.

While it was winter outside, her scent was summer—honeysuckle and heat. He cursed the leap his heart made into a faster rhythm. Victoria was off-limits. Sir Hawkins was his employer. No, he was more than that. He was both mentor and a father figure. Sir Hawkins had plucked him out of poverty and deprivation. It was not being melodramatic to say Garrick owed Sir Hawkins his life and livelihood.

The cynical part of Garrick that had blossomed in the orphanage understood the way Sir Hawkins had saved him meant his loyalty to the man knew no bounds. It was a wise, if cold-blooded, ploy on Sir Hawkins's part.

Would Sir Hawkins mourn if one day Garrick lost his life in service to Crown and country? He thought so, but Sir Hawkins would replace him within the week nonetheless. Garrick alternatively admired and despised the pitiless mentality Sir Hawkins possessed.

Victoria released his arm and stepped to the opposite side of the study door. He opened and closed his hand, flexing his forearm, the ghost of her touch branding him and applying a spark to the tinder of attraction simmering between them. As usual, he ignored it.

Victoria smiled. Not a polite, simpering smile. He wasn't sure she even had the skill for such. Her smile was one of such warmth and energy that blood hummed through Garrick as if he'd downed a carafe of Arabian coffee.

Had Garrick ever seen Sir Hawkins smile out of simple happiness? He stifled a guffaw at the thought. Sir Hawkins was not a sunny, happy man. And neither was Garrick. He didn't have the luxury of happiness. Life was a struggle and mostly unfair, and nothing in his recent experience had contradicted that theory.

Yet Victoria's mere existence proved there was light and goodness and beauty in the world. How some London dandy hadn't snapped her off the marriage mart was a great mystery of the universe.

He resumed his stance of casual alertness, and she mimicked him, propping her shoulder against the wall and crossing her arms. His gaze dipped to her décolletage, which her arms framed rather deliciously even though her bodice was modest. He snapped his attention back to her face.

"Thomas." No one called him Thomas but her. "You were lurking."

Her voice held a sultry, husky quality that hinted at a passion barely constrained by her innocence. How he envied the man who would have the honor of unleashing her ardor and nurturing her natural curiosity. The intimacy should not be allowed, yet he did nothing to correct her.

"I apologize for frightening you." He kept his voice low and soothing. "However, I wasn't lurking. I was standing here clear as day, but you were woolgathering."

"I wasn't paying attention to my surroundings. Father would be disappointed in me." The look she cast him through her lashes was unintentionally flirtatious. Or was it intentional? His ruminations on the possibility were interrupted when she asked, "Has Father tasked you with holding up the wall for the duration of the day?"

"I shall endeavor to keep it from toppling upon your head."

"That seems like a waste of your considerable talents." Her gaze flicked across his shoulders and chest, and his muscles tensed in response. "But I imagine you will do an admirable job."

What did the gleam in her eyes mean? Was she comparing him to the foppish men who came to call on her in their tailored frock coats? Most of them had never known a day of real labor. How did he measure up against the gentlemen of her acquaintance?

In his line of work, brawn was an asset, and while Garrick hadn't been gifted with breeding or luck, he had brawn in spades. He was taller than most men, many inches taller than Victoria, and held no illusions as to his looks. His nose had been broken his first day in the orphanage as a welcome from the older boys. Every time he stared into the looking glass, the crook was a reminder of how quickly happiness could be snatched away.

Unlike some of his comrades, he would never be called upon to don proper attire and pass for a gentleman. He was known as Hawk, the silent protector.

"Is Father working at the house today?" Victoria tucked a springy curl behind her ear.

"He is in his study," Garrick said vaguely. Sir Hawkins was secretive and tight-lipped, and even Garrick never knew what to expect from day to day. He'd learned to think on his feet and be prepared for anything.

"I suppose you know we have been invited to a yuletide house party by Mr. and Mrs. Barclay at their manor in Bedford-shire. Will you be accompanying us?"

"I should think not." While he'd spent years in Hawkins's household, he wasn't part of the family. Yet he wasn't a servant either. Much like his old tutor, Garrick was caught between worlds.

Sir Hawkins had made sure Garrick's education was well-rounded and in depth, covering mathematics, history, and weaponry. Not altruistically, of course. Sir Hawkins had reaped the rewards of Garrick's skills many times over since war with France had broken out.

A crinkle appeared between Victoria's eyes. "Please tell me Father is not sending you off somewhere distant and dangerous."

"I don't believe so, but..." Garrick shrugged. If Sir Hawkins had plans for him, he wasn't aware of them.

"I worry one day you won't come home." Victoria bit the fullness of her lower lip and met his gaze squarely.

It wasn't unusual for Garrick to return from missions a bit bruised and the worse for wear, but he hadn't known Victoria noticed. A vulnerability and awareness of their difference in station hit him like a punch to the chest. "This isn't my home."

A puzzled look crossed her face. Of course Victoria was aware he'd been orphaned, but he'd never discussed his parents. His life was defined as before and after the tragedy, and even though years had gone by, the loss had the ability to eviscerate his lungs and make it difficult to draw a steady breath.

"But where will you spend the yuletide?"

"I expect I'll remain in London."

"Have you… friends in town to make merry with?" The slight hitch in her voice was a chink in her usual confidence.

"Of course." *Lies.* He couldn't name a single person he would feel comfortable calling upon socially. Agents of the Crown made for terrible friends. None of them trusted one another. It was difficult to make merry when constantly on guard against a double cross.

"I see." Her gaze skated away from him.

What did she see? He wanted to take her by the shoulders and force her to look at him, to strip away the polite, slightly distant facade they'd erected two years ago. Ever since— No, he couldn't allow himself to revisit their brief moment of madness.

At least not while standing within arm's length of her. The temptation to engage in another bout of madness was all too strong. He would only allow himself to relive every glorious, agonizing second at night in bed. Alone.

He couldn't afford entanglements of any kind. His solitary existence was a necessary part of his job. Emotional ties could be manipulated and twisted until desperate choices were forced to be made.

By comparison, Victoria's social circle was extensive. All

manner of ladies came to call in the afternoons, young and old, peeresses and cits. Victoria was the sun, drawing others into her orbit like planets. She could converse on fashion and politics with equal insight. Ladies tripped over themselves to have her ear. It was unfortunate Sir Hawkins didn't possess his daughter's charm to coax secrets directly from their sources.

"I'm looking forward to leaving London for the country air. I'm tired of choking on coal smoke," Victoria said, her own tone turning as brisk and cool as the winter's wind.

"Won't you miss the merriments of town?"

A shadow darkened her features before her lips quirked in a small, wry smile. "I will welcome the change in scenery and hopefully find some peace. I confess, even in December, I find London exhausting."

The hairs on his nape wavered. His natural instincts had been honed by years of confronting subterfuge. What—or who —was she looking to escape? "Is there something amiss?"

"Of course not." Once more, she avoided meeting his eyes.

She was lying. Or at least not being entirely forthcoming. That Victoria enjoyed a bit of subterfuge was no secret to him, but her sojourns to bookshops and museums in the disguise of a plump, veiled widow in black were harmless. Or was she more like her father than Garrick wanted to believe? Was she dallying in more serious deceptions? He did not enjoy the off-balance feeling the thought gave him.

Lady Hawkins poked her head around the morning room door. While she was petite and delicate-looking, she had ambition and intellect to rival her husband. At the moment, her focus was centered on matching Victoria with a peer in hopes of their family rising another rung in society, and he had no doubt she would succeed. Lady Hawkins and Garrick got on like a hen tolerating a mutt as long as he kept the foxes at bay.

"Come and have tea while it's hot, Victoria. We have an appointment with the modiste in an hour. How are you this morning, Garrick?" Lady Hawkins asked in a way that indicated polite disinterest.

"It's a fine, brisk day, ma'am, with bright blue skies." Garrick inclined his head. "And how are you?"

"Tolerably well." A smile didn't mar the stern lines of Lady Hawkins's face, and her nod was perfunctory. "You take care of yourself and Sir Hawkins too."

"You can count on me, ma'am."

Lady Hawkins made a harrumphing sound, but the lines etched along her forehead smoothed. She retreated but left the morning room door cracked.

If anything happened to Sir Hawkins, Britain would be at a great disadvantage in the chess game of war. It was Sir Hawkins, and not Wellington, who deserved the accolades, but the world at large would never know his name.

Instead of rushing to do her mother's biding, Victoria tarried with Garrick. The undercurrents between them ruffled his calm like a hand rubbing a dog's fur the wrong direction. "What's amiss?" he asked again, this time with more vehemence.

Her lips moved slightly, as if words were desperate to form themselves into a confession. She finally shook her head and smiled a bright, sunny smile that didn't banish the shadows in her eyes, and her voice took on a falsely blithe lilt. "What on earth could be amiss? I'm to get a new frock this morning."

With that, she glided away. But before she disappeared into the morning room, she glanced over her shoulder, and their gazes clashed like flint. Fingers of sensation tiptoed down his spine as she disappeared.

STILL LOOKING over her shoulder at Thomas, Victoria tripped over the rug and caught herself on the small breakfast table set for two. The bump made the china cups clatter in their saucers.

Her mother shot her a glance over the top of the morning paper but returned to reading without commenting on Victoria's unusual clumsiness.

Victoria had almost told Thomas about her complication. No, it had been a complication a fortnight ago. Now it was bordering on a full-fledged catastrophe. Why had she involved herself in someone else's love affair?

It was easier to blame her penchant for novels than her naivety. It had seemed romantic and harmless to be the go-between with letters and notes to and from Lady Eleanor Stanfield and Lord Berkwith. Yes, Eleanor's parents had forbidden the match, but Victoria thought Lord Berkwith charming, not unattractive or old, and in love with her friend. She had been happy to help nurture the tendresse.

Victoria hadn't expected the tendresse to progress to talk of an elopement. Second—and third and fourth—thoughts had sprouted after subtle questioning had revealed Lord Berkwith had amassed a large debt gambling. Victoria couldn't fathom how that much could be lost in a single year. Was the gleam in Lord Beckwith's eyes when they alit upon Eleanor true love or avarice?

Victoria drank her tea and pushed the runny yolk of her egg around her plate with a triangle of toast. Her stomach was a mass of nerves, and not all of them could be attributed to Eleanor's romantic entanglements. An unholy number of them were because of the man standing outside her father's study only a few feet away.

Thomas Garrick. The man was a cipher. He exuded a raw physicality some found intimidating but she found darkly attractive. He was nothing like the gentlemen who danced attendance on her at London's social gatherings, because he wasn't a gentleman. His solid grip on her arm was evidence of that. She rubbed the place he had touched, her skin still tingling.

His dark eyes were calculating yet kind. And his voice... The deep silk was luxurious and mesmerizing and invited her to confess all her secrets. Secrets that went beyond promises made to a friend. Secrets like dreams where she woke tangled in her sheets, her body longing for Thomas to escort her through the door he'd cracked open with his kiss. The memory was nearly two years old, but heat still flushed through her until she wished for a fan in December.

At the time, she'd hoped it would be the start of something. Instead, her hopes had been cruelly dashed. Despair scuttled over her like clouds muting the sun. He would never kiss her again. A terrible mistake, he had called it. A moment of weakness from a man who was never weak.

She was twenty. It was time to leave her childish fantasies and dreams behind and choose someone suitable. Her mother was pushing her to marry into the ton. An heir to a title was out of her reach, but a second or third son would be a coup. Her father, on the other hand, would prefer her to choose a well-connected man with political aspirations.

As for herself… She wanted the one man she could never have.

"What were you and Garrick discussing so intently?" Her mother eyed her over the paper as if she could see straight into the maelstrom of Victoria's thoughts.

"Nothing." The knee-jerk response came out like a defensive jab. Victoria cleared her throat, dropped a sugar cube into her tea, and stirred. "That is to say, nothing of import. Only our plans for yuletide. I asked Thomas where he planned to bide his time."

Her mother's mouth tightened as if readying a lecture on the improper use of Garrick's given name. It was an old argument, and one Victoria had long ago won. Her mother snapped the paper in annoyance but only said, "Harold probably has some errand for the boy. I'm sure he prefers to stay busy seeing as he has no family to speak of."

"He has us," Victoria said hotly.

Too hotly based on her mother's glare. "Your father acquired Garrick to fill a position. He should be grateful he was not forced into manual labor or worse."

Victoria bit her tongue. Her mother had always been sensitive to Thomas's position. If Lady Hawkins had provided her husband with a son, Thomas would not have played such a prominent role in their household. It was a wound that pained her mother and manifested as a muted resentment toward Thomas.

Victoria regarded her mother over the rim of her teacup. "Perhaps he would have been better off doing an honest day's work instead of the skullduggery Father requires."

While they engaged in a tacit agreement not to discuss Sir Hawkins's duties, Victoria was not dense. Men—and sometimes women—with the same hard edge as Thomas arrived at all hours during the day and night bearing messages. Thomas occasionally disappeared and returned battered and bruised, a haunted, hunted look reflecting from the obsidian depths of his eyes.

"Garrick is better educated than any man of his station. He was lucky your father recognized his potential." Her mother folded the paper and did not meet Victoria's eyes, which said more than the platitude she offered.

Victoria supposed there was some truth to it. Thomas had come to them as a tall, gangly, underfed fourteen-year-old clutching a sackcloth of meager possessions. She'd been eleven, pudgy and fearless, yet lonely as an only child.

Thomas had done his best to ignore her, concentrating on excelling in his studies with a desperation she didn't understand then. His disinterest in her hadn't mattered. She had been smitten. Thomas had imprinted on her at a precarious time and awakened something inside of her that could never be caged again.

A sudden thought made her heart catch. Did he have a special friend to spend the yuletide holiday with? A *lady* friend?

"Victoria." The admonishing way her name was spoken made Victoria look up like a hare hearing the bark of a hunting dog. Had her mother guessed the bent of her thoughts? "We need to discuss your future."

"Do we?" Nerves sizzled in her stomach.

"Your second season ended without an offer."

"It did indeed," Victoria said with trepidation. It was a fact she couldn't dispute.

"You have many boon companions that come to call, your dance card is always full, yet no gentleman has caught your attention or earned your encouragement."

"No, I suppose not." The direction of the conversation felt dire. "Are you growing impatient to have me settled in my own household?"

Her mother's sigh was more than slightly frustrated. "Don't you want your own household? Don't you dream of having children?"

Victoria imagined herself waiting for her husband to return from his ventures while mending his socks. It seemed dreadfully dull. And children? She'd never spent much time in their company, but from her observations while walking in the park, they were loud and usually on the grubby side of cleanliness. Not the stuff of dreams.

However, she couldn't fault her mother's line of questioning. It was reasonable considering her age and the amount of money her parents had spent on presenting her to London's finest citizens. No, the trouble with her mother's question was Victoria couldn't picture a husband.

The gentlemen she'd met over the past two seasons had not inspired any sort of passion. In fact, the wide-eyed romanticism instilled by her reading was slowly but surely transforming into a more jaded view of men. The longer she was on the marriage mart, the more she felt like cattle. Instead of a dance card, presenting her breeding credentials and her dowry to the ha'penny would save everyone time.

"Of course I would like to marry and have my own household?" False enthusiasm turned her answer into a question. She should be a better liar, considering her father was an artist in the medium. Something to ponder another time. "To be honest, I haven't met a gentleman who stirs my senses."

"Your senses?" Her mother tipped her head and regarded Victoria for a long moment like a scientific experiment gone wrong. "You should not rely on your *senses* to choose a husband. Your senses will betray you. Marriage is a structure that will provide you and your children security. If you choose wisely."

"What about love?"

Her mother's smile held a ghostly sadness that lived in a past Victoria wasn't privy to. "Love is fleeting. Love won't keep you warm and fed and comfortable."

Had her mother's heart ever skipped a beat and her breath caught when her father entered a room? "Did—*do*—you and Father love one another?"

"Your father and I rub along well enough." Her mother rose, and Victoria did the same, leaving them facing off over an audience of kippers. "I want you to become serious about seeking a husband, Victoria. That was my point of this conversation. The Barclay's house party will be an opportunity for you to make a choice."

"You want me to pick a husband during a week-long house party?"

"Several suitable men you are already acquainted with will be attending. Lord Crenshaw, for instance. Although he is only a baron, his holdings are respectable, and he has an interest in politics."

"Lord Crenshaw is an insufferable popinjay who is twenty

years older than I. We would never suit." All the excitement of the house party was being stomped to bits.

Her mother's gaze dropped to look the kippers in the eye instead of Victoria. "If not him, what about Lord Percival? He's not much older than you. A third son, but I've heard he will receive a generous living."

"He's nice enough, I suppose." Victoria couldn't imagine facing off with Lord Percival over the breakfast table every morning. He was as bland and boring as a water biscuit. Palatable, but not tempting in any way unless nursing an upset tummy.

"Such a match would offer you a future and protect you. Your father is in agreement."

"Father wants me gone? He believes I need protection?" Her father had never voiced an opinion on who did or did not court her. In fact, her father rarely accompanied them on social occasions, and when he did, he often departed early. He had hitherto shown no interest in her marriage prospects beyond providing a modest dowry and coin enough for a suitable wardrobe.

Her mother leaned over the table. "You are strong willed and independent."

"You speak as if those are not admirable traits."

Her mother's face could only be described as exasperated. "Gentlemen prefer docile, agreeable wives."

"Perhaps I shouldn't marry a gentleman then." Victoria crossed her arms, her mood nearing an all-out sulk. "You aren't a docile, agreeable wife, and Father doesn't seem to mind."

While it wasn't the nicest of phrasing, it was perfectly truthful. In contrast to her delicate frame, her mother had a stalwart personality and tended to run roughshod over anyone who disagreed with her.

Her mother cleared her throat and tried a smile that did nothing to assuage the dread settling on Victoria's shoulders like a shawl weaved of maternal expectations and crushed dreams.

"Let's not argue. We have an appointment to keep. I'll call for the carriage." Her mother swept out of the room.

The ticking of the clock was a grim accounting. How much time did she have before her life was at the mercy of a husband she would have little say over choosing? A knife of resentment was at her throat.

Despite her reservations, she promised herself to do whatever it took to help her friend Eleanor attain the happiness that felt out of reach for herself.

CHAPTER 2

*G*arrick nodded at the man who slipped out of Sir Hawkins's study like a wraith. It was the only acknowledgment given or received. Names meant nothing to the agents who came and went. They could be slipped on and off like a hat.

"Garrick," Sir Hawkins called out.

Garrick pushed himself off the wall and entered the study. Sir Hawkins was seated behind the desk writing a missive. His movements were economical, but Garrick noted an unusual fitfulness in the way he signed his name. Remaining silent, Garrick stood and waited, his hands behind his back.

"I want you to accompany Victoria and Lady Hawkins on their errands this morning." Sir Hawkins didn't look up as he blotted his note before folding and sealing it with wax.

"Why?" Garrick narrowed his eyes. He wasn't asking to be difficult but because something had obviously happened to prompt the unusual request. "You don't trust Henry and Callum?"

The footman and groom who usually accompanied the Hawkins ladies on their outings had been trained by Garrick himself. They were capable of defending themselves and the ladies.

"The longer the war drags on, the greater the unrest grows." It was a typically cryptic thing for Sir Hawkins to say, but Garrick didn't discount the network of men and women and even children who passed whispers to Sir Hawkins. Some solidified into truths, and some dissipated like smoke.

"Have threats been made against Miss Hawkins or Lady Hawkins?" Garrick's shoulders tensed and pulled the fabric of his jacket taut.

"Not precisely." Hawkins was often infuriatingly vague. "But I would feel more at ease if you were to accompany them in the carriage and remain at their side as they shop. Can I count on you?"

"I would protect Miss Hawkins with my life," Garrick said with more emotion than he intended.

Sir Hawkins looked up and stared at Garrick without blinking. It was quite unnerving. The urge to shift on his feet became a compulsion he barely halted.

Becoming aware not so much of what he'd said but what he hadn't said, Garrick added hastily, "And Lady Hawkins, of course."

"Of course." A gleam flashed in Sir Hawkins's eyes, but as the rest of his face was bland, Garrick didn't know how to interpret it.

"I'll watch for anything out of the ordinary and report back, sir." Garrick turned on his heel, exited the study, and tamped down any anticipation at spending the morning in Victoria's company.

This was not a carefree outing with a lady he might be more than slightly in love with. The mere thought must be eradicated. It was impossible.

After having a word with Callum and Henry, Garrick waited at the curb beside the carriage for the ladies, hands behind his back, his body still. Lady Hawkins descended the front stairs and treated him like a lamppost, ignoring his presence entirely.

Victoria was halfway down before she looked up and noticed him. The shadows casting worries across her face were banished by her radiant smile. For him. He smiled back. The muscles in his cheeks protested the rare usage.

Lady Hawkins entered the carriage with Callum's help. Victoria took the last steps slowly, her gaze never leaving his. She had donned a brown fur-lined pelisse with matching collar and cuffs. Her gloves were brown kid, and a reticule in the same yellow as her dress swung from her wrist. Springs of her black hair had escaped her bonnet to frame her face. The untamed wildness suited her.

He stepped forward before Callum could offer his hand. With no hesitation, she slipped her hand into his. Time splintered. The world spun on around them, but all he could see and feel was her. Such a simple thing, yet lightning arced between them.

After avoiding her for two years, they had touched three times in one morning. It was too much. Or was it not enough? Her thumb skimmed over the back of his hand with an unmistakable pressure. He tried not to read anything into the touch, but his fingers answered the call and clasped hers tighter. Even as he cataloged the delicacy of her hand, he noted her strength.

Then she was inside the carriage, and he drew his empty hand into a fist as if he could hang on to the feel of her. He swallowed and shook himself free from the spell she'd cast over him. He wasn't here to play patty-fingers with Victoria. He had a duty to perform.

He looked up and down the street, taking careful note of the other carriages and a man strolling in a black hat and swinging his cane. Nothing struck him as out of the ordinary. After giving Callum a nod, he joined the ladies in the carriage on the opposite squab. Callum would ride with the coachman, and Henry on the back. Each of them carried a pistol.

The interior of the carriage was dim after the unusually bright sunshine of the day. It wouldn't last long. Stacked clouds portending snow loomed on the horizon. The carriage jolted forward. Lady Hawkins continued to ignore him and stared at the passing scenery.

London wasn't crowded this time of year. Most of the ton had retreated to their country houses long ago, but a few families remained in London through the yuletide season if they couldn't garner an invitation elsewhere or had business in town like Sir Hawkins.

"Why are you accompanying us?" Victoria tilted her head, her gaze fixed on him. "Have you developed a keen eye for ladies' fashions, then?"

"I have many talents." He kept his face bland. "Or so I've been told."

The corners of her mouth twitched with puckish charm.

The memory of how soft and supple her lips had been and probably still were—not that he would get the chance to verify —was distracting him. He forced his gaze from her mouth to the window. Distractions were deadly. Even ones as tempting as the coveted memory of their one and only kiss.

"There's naught to worry over," he said.

"Who said I was worried?" While the sentiment was light-hearted, her voice was heavy.

He shot her a look, but it was her turn to stare out the window. Her profile gave none of her true thoughts away. He had no right to her confidences, but he was a patient man. It was one of his strengths. He would wait and watch and do whatever he could to help relieve her burdens.

The carriage pulled to a stop. Garrick didn't wait for Callum to open the door. He did it himself, positioning his bulk in the opening to protect Lady Hawkins and Victoria from possible threats. He made a quick study of his surroundings.

Two gentlemen stood in conversation farther down the street in front of a shop, but neither glanced at the carriage. Another man exited the shop next door and turned the collar of his greatcoat up against the chill, heading in the opposite direction. A hack clattered past, pulled by a run-down nag, the jarvey buttoned up tight and wrapped in a scarf against the brisk wind.

Garrick hopped to the curb and lowered the steps. Callum backed up to stand to the side of the modiste's door, his cheeks ruddy from the cold, his expression alert to trouble. Lady Hawkins descended first, her hand lightly touching Garrick's forearm for balance. Black hair streaked with gray peeked out of her bonnet. She had the same curls as her daughter, but she kept them under strict control, while Victoria's rebelled, as if drawing from her personality.

Victoria slipped her hand into his again, her grip firm. Her gaze remained on her feet, and he caught the flash of her stocking-covered calf above her half boots as she descended. He swallowed and released her with difficulty. The barrier he had arduously erected between them after their kiss had been demolished by the mere touch of her hand and flick of her hems.

Callum opened the door to the modiste, and Garrick trailed the ladies in. He felt like an invader. The land was as foreign as when he'd entered Portugal under the cover of darkness for the first time, unsure of the topography and ignorant of the language.

Ribbons and laces and fabrics in a rainbow of colors and patterns covered the walls and tables. His gaze darted, as if threats lurked behind every scrap of satin. It finally landed on Victoria, who was looking up at him with barely suppressed laughter. At his expense, of course.

"Would you rather wait outside with Callum?" The sparkle

in her eyes lit embers in his chest, warming him better than any hearth.

"Yes, I would, but I promised your father not to let you out of my sight." It wasn't exactly what he had promised, but it was a good excuse to torture himself and wallow in her presence for as long as possible.

He sidestepped to a rare open spot along the wall and did his best to disappear between a blue twill and a white satin.

"That will be difficult. Unless you plan on watching my fitting? I will be obliged to strip down to my shift." Victoria cocked her head and looked up at him through her dark lashes. "It would be quite scandalous."

His imagination took flight. What he wouldn't give to see Victoria stripped from her gown. Her limbs would be pale but lithe. Her breasts full and supple, her nipples— He clipped the wings of his thoughts before something embarrassing took place in his breeches.

Was she toying with him on purpose? Did she understand the magnitude of her power over him? He narrowed his eyes. Her color was high, and she fidgeted with the ties of her reticule. She didn't appear gleeful in her teasing. In fact, if he had to put a word to her mood, he would pick nervous.

Lady Hawkins sent a pointed look in their direction. Victoria left his side to discuss whatever ladies discussed with their modistes. They disappeared behind a curtain. Garrick checked in with Callum, who had noted nothing unusual, and then returned to the shop to wait. The young girl behind the counter kept tossing him glances. He was probably making the poor chit nervous. He ignored her.

What was taking so bloody long? He sidled closer to the curtain, taking care not to touch the delicate fabrics or laces along the way. Murmuring voices and Victoria's husky laugh reassured him. No one had spirited her away.

Someone on the other side of the partition ruffled the velvet curtain on their way past. The movement shifted the fabric enough to reveal a narrow slit. Instinct took over, and Garrick focused on the scene beyond as if he were observing a clandestine meeting between his enemies.

His breath caught the same time his blood rushed faster, leaving him light-headed.

Victoria stood on a raised dais facing a tall looking glass. She wore a gown of evergreen. The sleeves were long and tightly fitted, but the bodice scooped enticingly low, revealing the top curves of her breasts. Vines and red berries were embroidered along the hem, cuffs, and the edge of the bodice. She had cast her bonnet aside, and her curly hair wisped around her face and down her nape in an artlessly sensual fashion.

"Are you sure the gown is not too revealing, Madame Beauvoir?" Lady Hawkins asked. "We don't want the gentlemen at the house party to assume Victoria is desperate for an offer."

"Even if she is, eh, my lady?" Madame Beauvoir's French accent was fake, although well done.

If Garrick had to guess, the dressmaker was from the north of England. But who was he to begrudge a woman a new identity in order to make a living? Based on the concoction she'd fashioned for Victoria, the modiste was talented.

"The gown is tasteful and will draw the sort of attention you seek," Madame Beauvoir said.

"I love it, Mother." Victoria twirled and looked over her shoulder at herself in the looking glass.

"The color is quite becoming on you, dear. Wrap it up and have it delivered once the hem is adjusted, if you would, Madame Beauvoir."

"It will be finished by this afternoon. Miss Hawkins can wear it to your evening's entertainments, if she so desires. Would you like to order matching gloves and stockings?" The modiste and Lady Hawkins shifted to the side to discuss particulars while a young girl began undressing Victoria.

Garrick swallowed. He should look away. Their banter earlier had been in jest. Victoria's life was not in any danger. His sanity, on the other hand, was being held at gunpoint. Victoria remained facing him as the girl worked the length of buttons in the back. The bodice began to gape and reveal more delectable skin and the gathered edge of a white shift.

Victoria ran her hands along the skirts, then looked up with a smile when the girl gently tugged one of the sleeves down. Her gaze swept over the slit in the curtain, and he pressed himself back against the wall out of sight.

If he'd been in the field, the possibility of exposure would have signaled his immediate retreat. A wise agent knew when to give up a position, no matter how tempting the information gleaned could be.

All wisdom deserted him. He peeked through the slit once more, expecting her to have turned and shielded herself from the inappropriateness of his spying, but she hadn't. His position hadn't been compromised.

The girl had tugged both sleeves off and was helping Victoria step out of the heavy skirts. Her posture offered a tantalizing view of the shadowy valley between her breasts. She straightened on the dais, her shoulders back, her gaze finding its way unerringly to his, unflinching and brazen.

He had been outflanked. Not only was she aware of his attentions, but she welcomed them. Her breathing paced his, shallow and rapid, the movement drawing his attention downward along the tempting curves of her body. Her stays pressed her full breasts high. The rise and fall of her chest against the thin fabric of her shift was decadent. Her nipples were barely covered, and he ruminated on their shape and color.

Her waist dipped above the curve of her hips, and the looking glass reflected her pert bottom. The shadow of her mons was visible through her shift. He allowed his gaze to wander all the way to her stocking-covered feet and then back up. In his mind's eye, he lifted her shift higher and higher, exposing her calves, her knees, her thighs until...

"Anywhere else you would like to visit, my dear? We won't be back until after the new year." Lady Hawkins turned to Victoria while the modiste took the dress and disappeared into what Garrick assumed was her workroom.

Victoria blinked once, then shifted to face her mother while the shop girl helped her back into her yellow dress. "I should like to visit the milliner next door."

Lady Hawkins hummed thoughtfully before saying, "This will be our fourth visit to the milliner in as many weeks. You have shown an unusually keen interest in bonnets lately, yet you never seem to have one on in the garden. Why is that?"

Garrick didn't hear Victoria's reply. He backpedaled toward the door, flummoxed by his lack of control and positively dumbfounded at Victoria's boldness. He tried to summon shame or regret or some emotion that would blunt the arousal humming through him but failed.

Victoria was an innocent. The kiss they'd shared had been her first. How could he forget the tentative movement of her lips on his, and her gasp when his tongue coaxed hers out to play? She hadn't known where to put her hands or what to do with the passion roiling through her like a storm.

Of course, that had been two years ago. Much could have happened since. Victoria wasn't one to deny her curiosity. The thought was demoralizing and painful. Feeling suffocated by gewgaws and fripperies, he pushed his way outside and took a deep, bracing breath. The cold air made his lungs prickle and tamped down the unwarranted shot of jealousy. Lady Hawkins exited the modiste, followed by Victoria. Her head was down, her bonnet shielding her expression.

"Everything in order, Garrick?" Lady Hawkins asked.

In order? His entire universe was in utter and complete chaos.

"Yes, ma'am." He inclined his head and didn't meet her eyes in case she possessed a sliver of her husband's uncanny ability to see through him to the image burned in his mind of her daughter wearing nothing but her unmentionables.

"We are paying a visit to the milliner next door." Lady Hawkins looped her arm through Victoria's, and this time he remained outside while the ladies did their shopping.

His only option was to scrub the picture of Victoria from his head. He could never touch her again. He banged his head back against the stucco wall, but she remained forefront in his mind. Even more worrisome, she was still firmly rooted in his heart.

CHAPTER 3

$\mathcal{V}$ictoria wanted to crawl under her covers with her boon companions—embarrassment and shame—for the rest of the day, but she couldn't. Eleanor was counting on her. Lord Berkwith had left a note with Mrs. Leighton, the milliner, and Victoria needed to pass it to Eleanor. It was Lord Berkwith who had suggested the friendly milliner as a go-between for Victoria, the other go-between.

The chain of communication was overly complicated because Lady Stanfield, Eleanor's mother, was a blue-blooded hunting dog on the scent of rakes and fortune hunters. She took her role of mother and chaperone with a zealousness reserved for nuns.

Eleanor was not even allowed to waltz—the position deemed too scandalous—much less take a carriage ride in the park or a turn in the garden with a gentleman. It was no wonder Eleanor, a spritely, curious young lady, was chaffing under the rigid control.

The romantic ruse had worn thin for Victoria, and she wanted nothing more than to cede the role of intermediary to someone else. Or, even better, she wished Lord Berkwith would court Eleanor as a gentleman should and win over her parents. *If* his intentions were honorable, which Victoria was beginning to doubt.

Thomas kept his distance on their brief walk to the milliner's shop. He had seen her nearly naked. Would she ever be able to look him in the eye again?

She could have shielded herself or turned away or even screamed when she noticed him at the narrow curtain opening. Instead, she had invited his gaze, and if she were being truthful, she had gloried in it.

Her skin had gone hot and cold and tingly, as if she could feel his fingertips grazing across her body. Even now, her breasts were overly sensitive against her stays, and her belly ached with a longing she didn't fully understand. But she understood it was scandalous.

The books she'd purchased as the dour widow McClain had offered knowledge in black and white, but hadn't prepared her for the kaleidoscope of feelings Thomas's attention had unleashed.

He hadn't looked away and had seemed as boggled in the aftermath as she had felt. Her heart skipped faster in anticipation. But of what? They would never be given the opportunity to act upon their attraction.

She entered the milliner's shop and glanced askance at the woman behind the counter. The two of them had performed this dance before. Mrs. Leighton was a beautiful widow in her thirties who held herself with an elegance that rivaled any duchess. Victoria always came away feeling gauche in comparison.

A confection made of netting and feathers perched atop Mrs. Leighton's smooth blond chignon. The hat was a fine advertisement of her talents and would be at home in any ton ballroom.

While Lady Hawkins moved deeper into the shop, Victoria

tarried over a straw bonnet decorated with delicate artificial poppy flowers. What should have been plain had been made special by Mrs. Leighton's artistry. The milliner swept from behind the counter and joined her in examination of the bonnet.

"It would suit you very well, miss. The color would highlight your dark hair." Mrs. Leighton touched one of the red flowers. Her lace gloves couldn't disguise the calluses earned from the delicate millinery work.

"It is a veritable work of art." In a softer voice, she asked, "Did he leave a message?"

Mrs. Leighton passed a tightly folded missive into Victoria's hand. She stuffed it into her reticule without looking at what Lord Berkwith had written on the outside. Before she could turn and join her mother, Mrs. Leighton caught her wrist in a tight grip.

"You know Randall doesn't truly love your friend, don't you?" Mrs. Leighton spoke through clenched teeth, her lips still curled into a smile. The force and tone of the words took Victoria back. As did the use of Lord Berkwith's Christian name.

"Actually, I don't know that." But she suspected the milliner was correct. The knot in her stomach tightened.

"She should beware." Mrs. Leighton let Victoria go and nodded as if the vagaries of men were known to Victoria.

It was clear Mrs. Leighton believed Eleanor was on the path to heartbreak. Victoria would have to decide whether to confess her own misgivings to her friend. A headache brewed. She joined her mother where she was trying on a black-and-white turban.

"I know turbans are all the rage, but I'm not sure if they suit me." Her mother pursed her lips and examined her reflection.

"I'm feeling rather peaked, Mother. I don't feel up to joining the Carlyles for dinner. Especially as we will be leaving for

Bedfordshire day after tomorrow." Victoria fake coughed into her handkerchief.

Her mother removed the turban. "I hope you haven't caught a cold. A red, runny nose would make for a poor impression at the house party."

"A honeyed tea and a quiet evening will set me to rights."

"Then let's get you home and bundled into bed with a water bottle."

Garrick didn't ride in the carriage with them on their trip home. He crammed himself on top with Callum and John Coachman. Victoria battled relief and disappointment. Callum helped them descend when they returned to the town house, and Victoria was in her room waiting for a tray of honeyed tea within minutes. She paced until her maid, Annie, delivered the tea and a hot before pulling Lord Berkwith's note out of her reticule.

She tapped it on the desk, staring at the Berkwith's red wax seal of crossed swords. Typically she would disguise Beckwith's notes in one of her own and send them to Eleanor with a footman, but this time she would take it herself. Lord Stanfield, a baron with a smallholding in Yorkshire, had taken a town house a short walk away, which was how she'd made Eleanor's acquaintance.

After finishing her tea, Victoria rang for her maid to inform her they would be calling on Eleanor, which wasn't unusual. Unlike her next request. "I'll wait for you in the mews. We'll leave from there."

"The mews, miss? Are you planning a visit to the reading room or the bookshop as well? Should we change your gown?" Annie blinked, her spectacles lending her a myopic, slightly confused expression at all times. This made for an excellent ruse. In reality, the girl was as sharp as a hatpin and Victoria's partner in crime when it came to unsanctioned forays. Annie's brother worked for Sir Hawkins in a more dangerous capacity, but courage and willingness to take risks ran in the family.

"No need to change. We are only paying a call on Lady Eleanor." Her skulking was because she wanted to avoid her mother and, even more so, dreaded bumping into Thomas. The buzzing embarrassment and arousal from their secret encounter at the modiste hadn't faded. In fact, the longer she dwelled on the heat in his gaze as she stripped to her unmentionables, the closer she came to spontaneous combustion.

"Yes, miss." Suspicions hid poorly behind the deferent acquiescence, and Victoria found herself blabbering on.

"I wish to check on Artemis. It's been too cold to ride recently." As excuses went, wanting to visit her horse was thin. One of the girl's eyebrows arched, and Victoria thought, not for the first time, that Annie was underutilized as a lady's maid, but she only nodded.

"Very good, miss. Let me clear the tray, and I'll be there straightaway." Annie gathered the tea tray and retreated to the kitchen.

Victoria slipped out the back with no one the wiser and did visit Artemis while she waited for Annie. It was better to keep her lies to a minimum. After Annie joined her, they set off at a brisk walk made brisker by the lowering temperature and reached the Stanfields' town house in less than five minutes. Annie went to the downstairs entrance to pass the time in the kitchens gossiping with the staff while the butler led Victoria to Eleanor, who was thankfully alone in the drawing room.

Eleanor took both of Victoria's hands in her own and pulled her to the settee. Eleanor wasn't a great beauty at first glance, but the longer one was in her company, the prettier she grew. Her hair was somewhere between blond and brown and stick straight. Her eyes were hazel and her lips thin, but her teeth were white and straight, and her laugh was simply infectious.

"You timed your visit with perfection. Mother just stepped

out to see to the packing. I'm so excited about the house party, aren't you?" Eleanor asked.

Considering she would be expected to make a life-altering decision while playing snapdragon, Victoria's enthusiasm had entered a downward spiral. "Indeed, but that's not why I called."

With more than a little trepidation, Victoria pulled the missive from her reticle. Eleanor snatched it from her hand, tore it open, and rose to stand by the window to read. She gasped and covered her mouth before looking at Victoria. Her shock was palpable.

"He... He wants me to elope with him," Eleanor whispered. "Tonight."

"What?" Victoria joined her friend and took the letter, scanning the contents. Beneath the flowery words of love and devotion lurked sinister undertones. Or so Victoria thought anyway. Mrs. Leighton's warning had only reinforced Victoria's instincts regarding Lord Berkwith.

"He implores you to meet him at the Bear and the Crown. That sounds like a common house or an inn. Ridiculous." If Lord Berkwith were standing in front of her, she would be tempted to employ a maneuver taught to her by none other than Thomas himself involving a well-placed knee.

"I shouldn't go. I can't go. Can I?" Eleanor's expressive eyes pleaded with Victoria, but she wasn't sure what answer her friend sought.

"I fear your dowry has induced this mad scheme."

"You don't believe he loves me?" Eleanor hugged herself.

Victoria opened her mouth to recount Mrs. Leighton's warning, but she swallowed the words. She didn't want to be the one to break Eleanor's heart. "If his love is true, he will be patient and woo you until your parents are won over. He shouldn't ask you to sacrifice your reputation."

"But he says he has given up his rooms and is spending the afternoon readying our conveyance. He will be waiting with bated breath for me, and I have no way to get word to him. His heart will be shattered if I do not meet him." Eleanor paced. "I can simply show up, inform him I can't elope, but my heart remains true, and return home."

"Your mother will never allow you take the family carriage to a common house. Alone. If you or your carriage are recognized, you will be ruined."

"Do you have a function tonight?"

"My parents are attending a dinner at the Carlyle's, but I begged off."

"Mother won't know that. I could tell her you have extended an invitation to me. She trusts Lady Hawkins. I will come to your house and once your parents have left take a hack to this Bear and Crown place and explain myself. Dear Randall will understand my heart is true. Then I will return to you with no one the wiser."

"That is a foolhardy plan. Not to mention dangerous. I can't support it."

Too many possibilities swirled. What if Lord Berkwith didn't take no for an answer and abducted Eleanor? As her father often opined, desperation turned good men evil, and Victoria wasn't sure how *good* Lord Berkwith was to begin with.

"You could send a note." Victoria knew the suggestion would be discarded before she even made it.

"I will go with or without your help." Eleanor's eyes gleamed with tears and determination.

It was clear Eleanor would not allow Berkwith to pine alone and discarded. Victoria paced and set to formulating a better plan—not that that was saying much. The last thing Victoria wanted was to involve herself further, but she saw no choice. At least she could take care of herself. Eleanor was an innocent lamb among wolves.

"I will go and decline the elopement on your behalf then call on you tomorrow with whatever message he would like to pass on to you." The one upside to her plan was being able to have a forthright chat with the possibly feckless lord.

"I can't ask you to put your reputation at risk for me, Victoria."

Victoria waved the thought away. "I am used to concealment and deception."

A puzzled look drew Eleanor's brows inward. "Whatever do you mean?"

Victoria pursed her lips. She'd said too much. For one thing, Sir Hawkins was only known as a man of political influence to society at large. Few understood his actual role. Not to mention, Victoria wasn't sure how Eleanor would look upon her clandestine outings to bookshops and museums dressed as a sober, veiled widow. Would she be fascinated or scandalized? Neither possibility boded well.

"You must be kind." Eleanor paced. "And you must assure him of my good will and affection."

"Of course, I'll be kind as possible." Unfortunately for Lord Berkwith, Victoria wasn't feeling a depth of human kindness at the moment.

"I wouldn't sleep a wink wondering at his reaction. No. I will tell Mother I'm accompanying your family to dinner this evening and wait in your room while you meet with him."

Victoria sighed and girded herself to persuade her friend otherwise. Fifteen minutes passed wherein Eleanor countered every argument Victoria made until she accepted it was useless. At least Eleanor would be safe in Victoria's room and not in Lord Berkwith's clutches.

On the walk back to her town house, Victoria worked out how to sneak Eleanor into her room, disguise herself, meet a man at a common house, and avoid getting caught or ruined. Honestly, it seemed straightforward enough.

∽

GARRICK COULDN'T SHAKE the niggling feeling something was wrong. Trouble was, he couldn't pinpoint the source as being external or somewhere in the vicinity of his heart.

He paced the pavement outside the Hawkins's town house, but the night was quiet. The temperature had dropped precipitously. The amassing clouds of the morning had moved in and obscured the moon and stars. The coal black sky spit out a few snowflakes.

He returned to the house, chafing his hands, and stood in the entry, hearing only the usual domestic clatter. The laughter from downstairs was a bit louder as the servants finished their work and socialized in the kitchen, knowing the master and missus were absent.

He'd been tasked to remain at the house. Victoria was feeling peaked, or so she'd informed her parents, and had bowed out of the planned dinner party. Garrick hoped he wasn't the reason she was feeling sick. The guilt of his indiscretion was crushing him. While he might not be well born or wealthy, he was honorable. Or so he'd believed.

A rattle of dishes brought his attention around to Annie, Victoria's maid. There was a steaming teapot, cup and saucer, and an assortment of food on a tray.

"How is your mistress feeling?" he asked.

The maid started and blinked at him. "She must be in poor straights. She asked me to leave the tray outside her door and not to enter under any circumstances."

"I'll take it to her. You can put your feet up in the kitchen." He took the tray. Or tried to, at any rate. Annie didn't seem inclined to let go.

"There's no need, sir. I'm sure you have more pressing matters." Annie tugged the tray back toward her.

"Annie. Let go of the tray." He used his most intimidating tone.

Annie firmed her jaw and, after another few seconds of

playing tug-of-war, released the tray with a rattle of china. "Have it your way, sir. But don't forget, Miss Victoria does not want to be disturbed. Just give a rap and leave the tray."

Nonplussed, Garrick stared at the maid. She seemed to be waiting for something, and finally, he nodded. "I won't disturb her."

"Very good then. See that you don't." Annie pointed a rather threatening finger at him before turning and making her way back toward the kitchens, reluctance obvious in her mincing steps.

He waited until she disappeared before tackling the stairs to Victoria's room. He owed her an apology. He should have offered one as soon as they'd returned, but he'd been a coward. He let a huffing laugh escape. He'd never been accused of cowardice before. His cohorts in the shadows would have a good laugh over his current predicament.

He hesitated outside Victoria's door before shifting the tray and rapping lightly. "Are you well?"

No answer.

"I'm going to come in. If you're truly ill, I should send for a physician."

A thump sounded on the other side of the door, followed by shuffling feet. "Uh, no, thank you, sir. I merely need sleep. Leave the tray outside and leave. Please."

Sir? Had Victoria ever addressed him such? Only mockingly, and the voice on the other side held no humor. Garrick examined the tray. Bread and cheese and cured meat. A hefty slice of cake. Whoever was on the other side of the door, it wasn't an ill Victoria. Was it a French agent? Was Victoria being held hostage or worse?

Garrick's heart sprinted ahead, but he forced fear out of his head. Noiselessly, he set the tray down and tried the latch. Locked. In as calm a voice as he could manage, he said, "I know you aren't Victoria Hawkins. Open the bloody door."

"Wh-whatever do you mean? Of course I'm Victoria." Whoever was in the room was too poor a liar to be an enemy agent.

"You have until I count to five to open the door."

"Or what?"

"Or I will break the door down and force the truth out of you. Very unpleasantly."

He made it to two.

A soft creak signaled her capitulation and revealed a lady who had come to call many times but whose name he couldn't recall. The bed was rumpled, and a novel lay splayed on the rug. Nothing else in the room raised alarms. Except for the woman who was not Victoria.

"Who are you?" he asked.

"E-Eleanor Stanfield. Lady Eleanor Stanfield." She shuffled backward until her bum hit the mattress, and she sprawled in a half-reclined position. "Please don't ravish me."

The lady was terrified, and as it was partly—all right, *mostly*—his fault, he tempered his voice and held up his hands in supplication. "I'm not going to ravish you. I've been tasked to protect Miss Hawkins by her father. I can't protect what is not here, now can I? Where is she?"

"Nowhere."

Garrick sighed. "Lady Eleanor. I know you know where she is. Tell me."

Lady Eleanor daubed her lips with her tongue, her gaze darting around the room as if the answer lay somewhere between the bed and hearth. "She's running an errand for me."

"This late in the evening? Unchaperoned?" His hands curled into fists.

Sir and Lady Hawkins had taken the carriage, which meant Victoria was traveling on foot or in a hack. While he didn't want to frighten Lady Eleanor into muteness, urgency thrummed through him. He stepped forward and stared into her eyes. "Victoria may be in danger. You need to help me help your friend. Where did she go?"

With the tell of one who was guilty, she couldn't hold his gaze. "The Bear and the Crown."

He was familiar with the common house. It sat on the edge of Clerkenwell, a section of London that had been fashionable many monarchs ago. It had deteriorated into a warren full of vendors and artists and printers. While it wasn't as dangerous as Seven Dials, it was no place for a gently bred young lady, even one as capable as Victoria, especially after dark.

"Why on earth did she go to the Bear and the Crown?"

"To meet a gentleman."

Her pronouncement made him reel back a step. Had he been blind to the fact she was in love with another? Had his blatant hunger driven her to rashness?

"I didn't realize she had a special gentleman." He barely recognized his voice. "Still it begs the question of why he is not calling at the house like a true gentleman."

"Oh. Well, as to that..." Lady Eleanor fiddled with the lace edging on her sleeve. "Lord Berkwith is not her special gentleman, but... mine."

"Victoria has gone to meet Lord Berkwith? On your behalf?" At Lady Eleanor's nod, he ran a hand through his hair. "Why would she do such a foolish thing?"

"She only wished to protect me. You see, Lord Berkwith asked me to elope with him." Now that the confession had begun, the words rushed out in a torrent. "Victoria didn't think it wise. She says he should pay his addresses like the gentleman he is, but I had no way to get a missive to him and didn't want him to think my love is not true, so Victoria went in my place."

He had many questions but distilled his thoughts to the most pertinent. "How did she get there?"

"She planned to walk until she came across a hack to hire."

"Did she take anyone with her?" Callum, Henry, and Annie

were all at the house, so he was terrified he already knew the answer.

"No," Lady Eleanor said in a small voice.

"When did she leave?"

"A quarter hour ago. Perhaps a bit less."

A heartbeat later, he was in motion, taking the stairs two at a time and running for the mews behind the town house. Garrick kept a horse stabled in case Sir Hawkins needed him on urgent business. He saddled the bay gelding in under two minutes and paused for a breath, considering leaving word with Callum, but every second felt precious.

Garrick swung himself into the saddle and pointed the horse toward Clerkenwell. The streets weren't crowded, and with any luck he'd make up time on her head start.

When—he didn't allow himself to think in *ifs*—he found her safe and sound, he was going to sit her down and tell her exactly what he thought of her.

The woman was daft and careless. Loyal and brave. Bold and beautiful. No woman had ever come close to usurping the ridiculous *tendre* he nurtured for her. He would kiss her again, and this time he wouldn't apologize.

Fear mounted. He had seen too much to assume she would be safe because she was a gentlewoman. In fact, as Sir Hawkins's daughter, she was in even greater danger.

CHAPTER 4

*V*ictoria squirmed on the squab. The springs dug into her bottom, and for the first time, she was thankful for the darkness and her veil so she couldn't see what smelled so musty. The passing town houses and shops grew more modest the farther they clattered away from her home in Mayfair until they teetered on the edge of squalor.

Fear urged her to call up to the jarvey to turn around and take her home. Fury at Lord Berkwith stilled the compulsion. That he would ask dear innocent Eleanor to meet him at a less-than-respectable common house was beyond the pale and cemented Victoria's doubt as to his character. She would ring a peal over his head until he begged for mercy. He deserved worse. The man was a bounder.

The hack slowed. Victoria twisted the ties of her reticule around her fingers. A small sheathed dagger was inside. She had donned a plain black dress with an equally plain cloak and a veiled hat to mask her identity. Padding around her middle concealed her figure and, along with the unfashionable attire, gave the impression of a plump matron.

She wasn't unused to clandestine excursions, but her

unchaperoned daytime jaunts to bookshops didn't inspire the nerves she battled tonight. They had been larks. If she'd been caught buying torrid novels, at worst, her mother would have berated her and attempted to crush her with maternal disappointment. Victoria would have risen from the ashes unrepentant.

Tonight's excursion held the risk of ruination. There would be no coming back from that if she were caught.

"We're 'ere, miss." The jarvey's voice was muffled by the knitted cowl around his neck.

The remnants of a storied past were still evident on the sign swinging unevenly outside the Bear and the Crown. All that was left were crinkled flakes of red and blue and white muted by coal dust and neglect. The inn was busy on the cold evening, and every time the door opened, light and noise poured out a welcome.

She exited the hack and looked up at the man, his form shadowy behind the veil. "I'll only be a moment. Will you wait?"

"It'll cost you extra." The man didn't look at her but held out his hand.

She slipped him the coins, not sure if it was too much or not enough, and waited for his brief nod. Then she faced the door and adjusted her veil as if it were a knight's visor. Even the false protection was welcome.

She slipped in the door of the common house and scuttled along the wall, scanning the room for Lord Berkwith. It wasn't difficult to spot the popinjay among the crows. Narrowing her gaze, she strode to the bar where he was drinking an ale, his shoulders hunched and his foot jiggling on the boot rail.

The man was nervous. Was he nervous that Eleanor wouldn't show or because if she did, he would have to put his dishonorable plans into motion?

Victoria tapped his shoulder when she would have preferred to knock him across the side of his head. He spun around and tried to take her hands. "Oh, Eleanor, my love. You came. How bright you are to assemble such a disguise."

Victoria slapped his hands away. "I'm not the object of your affection, my lord. Come with me." She didn't wait for a response, but spun on her heel and left the common room.

After the crowded warmth of the room, the cold cut all the deeper. In the time it took Lord Berkwith to walk from the common house to the curb, he had assembled his wits, such as they were. "Why didn't Eleanor come? Does she not love me?"

The man sounded truly despondent, which gave Victoria pause. "If you wish to pay your addresses to Eleanor, you need to call upon her father and do it honorably, not by invitation to a common house for an elopement."

"Lord Stanfield believes I only want her dowry."

"And don't you? If the rumors are true, you have debts, my lord, rather substantial ones." Victoria suspected the color flushing his face wasn't entirely due to the biting breeze swirling around them.

"I can't deny her dowry would be most welcome, but please don't judge my character based on my past actions. I have not crossed the threshold of a gaming hell since meeting Eleanor." He lay his hand over his heart.

Blast it. She was inclined to believe him. It would be easier if she could dismiss him as a cad, but her father had taught her that people couldn't be sorted into good or bad bins. "And what of Mrs. Leighton? Have you professed your love to her as well?"

"How do you...?" Lord Berkwith cleared his throat. His reaction had provided answer enough, but he continued anyway. "We shared brief dalliance that meant nothing. She is a lady of the world and understands the way of these things."

Victoria was inclined to disagree. Mrs. Leighton was a woman of feeling like any other, yet Victoria could do nothing for her. She would, however, protect Eleanor as best she could. "You must prove your steadfastness to Eleanor and your worth to her family. Patience and persistence are required. No more invitations to common houses or plans to elope, my lord. Are we clear?"

"Quite." Lord Berkwith's gaze narrowed as if trying to see behind the veil. Hopefully, the dress and cloak and padding gave the impression of an older lady. Someone stern and not to be crossed, like a beloved aunt.

Victoria turned toward the waiting hack. Shadowy movement from the mouth of the alley down the lane caught her attention. Two men were moving toward her and Lord Berkwith. They were no doubt headed to the warmth and comfort of the Bear and the Crown. Except…

They didn't speak to one another or call out a good evening. Their movements were silent and stealthy and swift. They reminded her of the men who sometimes came to meet with her father. By the time she recognized the danger snapping in the air, the men were upon them.

She opened her mouth to warn Lord Berkwith, but it was too late. One of the men came up behind Lord Berkwith and thumped a truncheon against his temple. He crumpled like a rag doll. A shot of fear had Victoria leaping into action. She made a run for the hack while fumbling for the dagger in her reticule. The ties were a complex puzzle she couldn't solve.

Her breathless scream was snuffed out by the gloved hand that came over her nose and mouth. A hard arm circled her torso and lifted her. Her feet dangled uselessly off the ground. She tried to kick the man behind her, but her efforts were puny without any leverage. Air was at a premium, and primal panic had her pulling at the man's wrist, any thoughts of escape secondary to the simplicity of taking a breath.

Her training dissolved in panic. She clawed at the man's arm and kicked and wiggled against him. He only tightened his hold and dragged her backward toward the alley. Her feet scrabbled for purchase. Her hat was knocked over her eyes. The inability to see ratcheted up her panic to histrionic levels.

She snatched her hat off and tossed it aside, the pain from the yanking pins miniscule compared to the burning in her lungs. The hack clattered away from the scene at a high rate speed. No doubt the jarvey knew better than to get involved. The men hadn't made enough noise to cut through the laughter and conversation buzzing out of the common house.

Lord Berkwith raised himself to sitting and held the side of his head. Their gazes locked. He goggled at the sight of her being dragged into an alley, but he didn't make a move to help her. With her hat off and her hair coming loose, he surely recognized her. She tried to scream again, but her lungs were bereft of air. Pinpricks wavered her vision, and weakness invaded her limbs.

Was this to be her end? The shadows of the alley swallowed them. There was no one to help her. No one to save her.

She would have to save herself. The element of surprise was her greatest weapon. If they believed her weak, perhaps she could mount an attack. She let go of the man's arm and went limp against him, working on the ties of her reticule. The man's hand loosened enough for her to take a gasping breath. She gripped the hilt of her dagger and waited for an opportunity to present itself.

A grunt sounded behind her. The hand on her mouth was gone. The arm crushing her lungs loosened, and she dropped to the uneven stones of the alley, falling to her hands and knees. For a moment she allowed herself the joy of filling her lungs with air. Then she gathered her wits and looked deeper into the alley.

The outline of a horse blocked the far exit. One of her abductors lay motionless on the pavers. The other was exchanging blows with a third man. The newcomer wore a greatcoat and a brimmed

47

hat of a serviceable variety. He grabbed her captor by a lapel and drove his fist into the man's face. Her captor's head snapped back into the brick wall. He sank to join his compatriot on the ground.

Victoria looked from the two unconscious brutes to the last man standing. Was he friend or foe? She scrambled to her feet, clutched the dagger in a defensive pose, and took a careful step backward toward freedom.

"Thank you for the assistance, but I need to be going now." She cursed the waver in her voice.

The man watched her take two more steps from where he stood in the shadows. Just when hope flickered in her chest, he made his move. She flipped the knife into a guarded position and slashed toward him. The dagger clattered to the pavers. He had her disarmed before she realized how he had done it.

"Not bad. It might have even worked on a common footpad." The growly voice was only too familiar.

She couldn't summon even an iota of indignation toward him. She stepped closer and he gripped her arms. Only his hawklike nose, tight-lipped mouth, and stubborn chin were visible under the brim of his hat. She fought the urge to pepper kisses over every inch of available skin. How would the stubble of his night-beard feel against her lips? She shivered, but not entirely from the cold.

"Of all the idiotic, foolhardy capers... What in bloody hell were you thinking?" he asked.

She *had* been foolish and idiotic. She'd been too confident in her ability to take care of herself and too naive about the threats lurking in the shadows. "How did you know?" she asked hoarsely.

"It didn't take much persuasion to get the information out of Lady Eleanor."

"You didn't frighten her to half to death, did you?"

"Only a quarter to death." The shard of humor was like a

lightning bolt during a storm. "Part of me wants to shake some sense into you. The risks you take, Victoria. You drive me mad."

He tightened his fingers around her arms, and she braced herself for the promised shaking. It never came.

He kissed her. So hard and fast, she didn't have a chance to even close her eyes. It wasn't a kiss laced with passion, but proof of something much deeper and more primal. They were alive, and that's all that mattered. She leaned into his chest and tipped her face to his, her lips glancing across his stubbled jaw, the rasp even more appealing than she supposed.

One of the men in the alley groaned and rolled over, shattering the strange intimacy of the moment. They each took a step away from one another, opening a chasm between them. She was in a dank alley with two men who wished to do her harm. Now was not the time to commit another folly with Thomas.

"Let me see if I can finagle some information, then we can depart this foul place." He nudged his chin toward his horse. The handsome, sturdy bay gelding stood perfectly still in the opposite mouth of the alley. He was as well trained as his master.

Victoria held her skirts to the side and tiptoed by the men, keeping as much space between her and them as possible. Thomas squatted next to the man who was stirring and lifted him by the lapels. His head lolled.

"Who sent you?" Thomas asked in a harsh voice.

The man only groaned. Thomas dropped the man back down and riffled through his pockets, coming up with empty sweet wrappers and a dented watch. He left the watch on the man's chest and searched the second man, who had not moved since collapsing.

Thomas stood and muttered to himself before turning to Victoria and his horse. He mounted, then held out a hand for her. She put her foot atop his and let him haul her up behind him. She was astride and circled her arms around him. "What about Lord Berkwith? He could be gravely injured."

"It would serve him right for picking such a place for a rendezvous with a lady, the bounder." Despite the sentiment and the cantankerous manner in which it was delivered, Thomas circled around the common house.

Lord Berkwith was gone.

Thomas grunted, his disgust palpable. "Strike that. He isn't a bounder but a cowardly arse. He didn't even attempt a rescue."

He pointed his horse away from the common house. The pace he set was almost leisurely. They clopped through a maze of side streets and alleys.

A half dozen turns later, Victoria was utterly turned around. "Are we almost home?"

Turning his head so his face was close to hers, his breath was a puff of white in the air. "It's too dangerous to return."

The implications were starkly clear. "You don't think those men were two ruffians looking for easy coin?"

"Did they riffle through Lord Berkwith's clothes for his valuables?"

The men had treated Lord Berkwith like an inconvenience. They'd been focused on her. She'd been followed. But why? "What did they want?"

"I don't know, but we have to assume it involves your father." He tugged on the reins, and the horse deftly turned down yet another narrow alley.

"Where will we go?"

"We'll stop to send a warning to your father."

It wasn't an answer, but Victoria didn't press him further. She trusted Thomas.

An hour passed. The tightly packed buildings of London gave way to cottages with fallow gardens and bare trees. Unimpeded by buildings, a brisk wind found its way beneath her collar and under her skirts. She huddled behind Thomas's bulk and shivered.

Clouds hid the moon, and no lanterns lit their way. Thomas didn't seem bothered by the darkness and navigated them to a small cottage with an untidy front garden. Brown weeds bent over in supplication to the cold, and a trellis covered in a leafless vine marked the entrance.

Thomas dismounted and helped Victoria off. Her bottom was numb, and her lower back ached from the unusual experience of riding astride and double. Garrick loosely wrapped the reins around the rotting fence post.

"Are we not staying?" she asked as she followed him under the trellis.

"Only long enough to get a note to your father." The pattern of his knocks on the door was complicated and unique.

"A secret knock? Isn't that rather obvious?" She shot him a look.

"It's simple but effective."

"Unless the enemy has infiltrated your safe house and is waiting for anyone with an overly complicated knock."

Thomas shifted toward her, and she mimicked his stance until they were face-to-face. "Do you think you know better than Britain's finest agents?"

"I think I possess enough common sense to point out the weaknesses of your system." She held his stare.

His lips twitched. "Touché."

Footfalls and a grumbling voice came from the other side of the door. It cracked open. A candle in an old brass holder was held aloft. The sudden light, as weak as it was, made Victoria squint. The man behind the light came into slow focus. He wore a dingy nightcap, a nightshirt of the same hue, and a claret-colored, threadbare banyan.

"Is that you, Hawk?" The man's blue eyes were highlighted by white eyebrows with hairs that hied off in all directions.

"It is. I need you to rouse one of the boys to run a note back to town."

"Who is the baggage with you?" The man gestured toward her with the candle. It wavered and was almost snuffed out.

"I'm not baggage," Victoria said tartly.

"She's no one of import," Thomas said, speaking over her.

She glared at him but didn't argue. Her clothes were dowdy, her hair was trailing out of its few remaining pins, and she was traveling with an unmarried man. Their host had every right to assume she was worse than baggage.

"Come in then. You know where everything is." The man handed Thomas the candle and retreated down the dark, narrow hall while Thomas led her into a small receiving room. While the grate was unlit and the room chilly, it felt comfortable compared to being outside.

She plopped into an armchair. A poof of dust tickled her nose and made her sneeze. Exhaustion crept over her and tugged her eyes nearly closed. The shuffle of paper and the scratch of a nib registered. Thomas was huddled over the small writing desk.

"I suppose you're writing in some elaborate code?" She was half teasing.

"Of course." He was deadly serious.

"Mother and Father were dining with Mr. and Mrs. Carlyle."

"Yes, I know. I am aware of all your father's plans."

"Are my parents in danger?"

Thomas was biting his lower lip in concentration. The paper he wrote on was small, the markings tiny. The missive could be easily concealed and, knowing her father, who enjoyed games of strategy and logic, would be difficult to decipher.

He hesitated a moment before finishing the note and blowing on the ink in the absence of a sanding pot. "Your father is always in danger. You know that."

She did, but she preferred to ignore the reality as much as possible.

Thomas straightened and rolled the message into a narrow cylinder an inch long. He rang a bell sitting on the desk. Less than a minute later, a lean youth dressed for riding entered, nodded at Thomas, and held out his hand. The message was slipped into a slit in the lining of his jacket.

"You know what to do?"

"Aye, guv'nor. It'll not take a quarter hour."

"Good."

The youth departed. Thomas turned to Victoria and shuffled closer to loom over her. She let her head fall back against the top curve of the chair and met his assessing gaze.

She shifted on the lumpy cushion and rearranged her padding. Thomas noticed everything yet had said nothing about her attire. "No interrogation about the way I'm dressed?"

"What happened to your hat?"

"It ended up on the ground. A pity. It was difficult to procure such a hideous headdress without Mother's knowledge." She was rewarded by the merest quirk of his lips.

"We must move on," he said gently.

She had been afraid he would say that. "Can't we rest a while here? It's safe enough, isn't it? After all, a secret knock is required for entrance."

Garrick's lips twitched one more, but a smile didn't crack his serious expression. "I assume the men we're dealing with wouldn't bother knocking. I should have killed them," he finished on a sigh.

The two men in the alley had been large and used to brawling, yet Thomas had dispatched them with an ease that was both admirable and fearsome. Victoria had no doubt he could have sent them to their maker. "Why didn't you?"

His gaze traveled her face before meeting her eyes. "Death is not something a lady should witness, but never doubt, if they had hurt you, I would have ripped them apart with my bare hands."

Thomas delivered the declaration with the coldness of a man who had killed to survive and would do the same for her. The thought would send a proper lady into a fit of vapors. It was clear Victoria wasn't a proper lady, because his vow of violence struck her as almost... romantic.

"Where will we go?" she asked.

"Somewhere I can protect you and keep you safe." His voice held a sharp, jagged edge.

Bands of warmth tightened her chest and made it difficult to speak. She wanted him to take her in his arms and lend her some of his strength. That wasn't all. She wanted to kiss him again and take her time doing it. A tug of his nape would be all it took to bring his lips to hers.

The guttering candle illuminated only half his face, casting his features in harsh lines and angles that weren't handsome in the soft, well-fed way of the gentlemen filling her dance cards. Instead, Thomas was arresting. She couldn't look away, and she stared at him like she'd lost her wits.

Maybe she had. Or perhaps the day's events had merely stripped away all pretense that she didn't desire him in every inappropriate way possible.

Before she could act on her desire, he straightened and held out his hand. Without hesitation, she took it and stood. He tightened his grip and brushed an escaped curl off her forehead with a bare finger. The touch was like striking flint.

"Do you trust me?" The rumble of his voice held a tentativeness she wouldn't have expected from him.

"I trusted you from the very first."

He'd arrived on their doorstep with wide, suspicious eyes, a too-lean frame, and ragged hair. She'd made it a habit to pop into his room with a basket of the best treats from the kitchen to share. Days accumulated into weeks by the time she had finally earned a smile. It had been her greatest accomplishment up until that point in her young life.

He nodded crisply, but the heat in his gaze warmed her from the inside out. "The sooner we depart, the sooner you can rest."

The warmth he inspired didn't last. Snowflakes drifted from the sky, and the shock of the cold made her breath catch. She assumed the same position astride behind Thomas, thankful his bulk blocked the wind, but it was too miserable to relax.

Their synchronized swaying in the saddle was a metronome ticking off the seemingly endless seconds. The pace changed, and Victoria poked her head from behind Thomas's back. They left the road and descended into a shallow gulley. The copse beyond was dark and menacing.

Victoria looked behind them. The snowfall had picked up in intensity and was already filling the divots made by the horse's hooves. In an hour, maybe even less, there would be no evidence of their passing. The horse chuffed and tossed his head.

"Are we close?" she asked.

"The cottage is just through the trees."

Victoria squinted but could only see a few feet in front of them. The trees thinned out, and the gurgle of a brook welcomed them. The faint outline of a thatched crofter's hut in a small clearing came into view. Thomas stopped at the edge of the trees and scanned the area.

After long seconds in which Victoria knew better than to ask questions, he proceeded across the shallow water. They dismounted next to a lean-to that had been erected against a hillock to block the wind.

Thomas nodded toward the hut. "Go on while I get him settled with water and oats."

Victoria wasn't going to argue. Her legs shook, and her feet were numb. She fumbled with the latch, the kid of her gloves damp from the snow, her fingers clumsy from cold. It wasn't much warmer inside the hut than outside, but she was thankful to be out of the wind.

Using her teeth, she pulled off her gloves and rubbed her hands together while her eyes adjusted. The outline of a lantern caught her eye. It had been left next to the door within arm's reach. She was surprised to find it full of oil. A flint lay next to it.

Welcome light burst from the wick. It was amazing what comfort such a mundane convenience as light could be. She held up the lantern and took stock of her surroundings. It was a small but neat little hut. Wood was stacked next to the hearth, a sturdy table and two chairs were against the far wall, and a bed piled with quilts was in the corner.

One bed.

Her mouth was suddenly bereft of moisture. No doubt Thomas would offer to sleep in the chair or on the floor like a gentleman. But... what if she didn't want him to be a gentleman?

She shoved the thought out of her head. They were on the run from men who had wanted to abduct her or worse. Her parents might be the next target, and she had no idea whether Garrick's note had found her father in time to take precautions.

The existence of one bed in the cottage should not be her primary focus. Yet she was still staring at the bed when the door opened and knocked her in the back, startling her out of her daze. Clearing her throat, she shuffled farther into the cottage with the lantern.

Thomas stamped his feet and shivered. "Once I start a fire, we'll warm up quickly."

"I should have done that." She refused to admit what had distracted her.

Thomas slid his great coat off, hung it on a peg next to the door, and squatted in front of the hearth, deftly laying wood and kindling. The crackle drew her closer, and she stood behind him, watching his big, capable hands limned in firelight as he tended the flame until it was a healthy blaze. Thomas rose and bumped her with his shoulder. She grabbed his arm to catch herself. The muscle was ropey with strength.

"Sorry," she murmured.

"My fault. The two us will have to manage the best we can in the small space, I'm afraid."

She slid her hand up his arm a few inches. While her physical balance was restored, the foundation of her neat, safe world had shifted. She should be safely in her room, her part in Eleanor and Lord Berkwith's love affair over once and for all. If she hadn't gone to the Bear and the Crown, the night would have passed like any other. She would have woken and begun packing for the sojourn to the house party, where her mother would expect her to settle on a suitable gentleman to wed.

The path of her life had diverged into a dark wood with a new companion.

"Thomas. My parents. Will they be safe?" She tilted her face to look him in the eyes, sure she would be able to detect truth from lie.

"Sir Hawkins is as wily and shrewd as any man I've ever met. Henry and Callum are well trained. I made sure of that. My note should have reached the right people in time. If there is a grander plot afoot, I have every confidence your father was given ample warning to avoid danger."

"I know Father courts peril every day, but I've always felt safe. Until now. Was it all an illusion?"

"You have been safe," he said vehemently and then sighed. "Until now. The French are growing desperate with each passing day. There are those in England sympathetic to Napoleon's cause and others who have profited from the war and do not want peace. Sir Hawkins holds the keys to many secrets. He is valuable, and you would be an excellent bargaining chip."

"Those men wanted me in order to force Father into betraying his country and mission?"

"It seems likely." His expression turned thoughtful. "If they had wanted to kill you, it would have been a moment's work to slip a knife between your ribs or slash your throat."

She touched her neck and swayed. Her shock must have reflected on her face. How close had she come to dying this night?

"That was badly done of me. I didn't mean—"

"Yes, you did. Never apologize for telling me the truth. I appreciate not being coddled." The room was warming, and she slipped off her cloak and hung it on a peg next to Thomas's. With her back to him, she asked, "What would Father have done if those men had succeeded in taking me? Would he have bowed to their demands?"

Thomas's hesitation was answer enough. "Sir Hawkins is your father. The rest of us see him as something different altogether."

"Even you?" She turned and regarded him with the same fascination and curiosity she'd always felt around him. "He saved you from the orphanage and educated you like the son he never had."

"A son?" He laughed, but it was full of bitterness. "I had a father. A good one at that. I never wanted another."

CHAPTER 5

*G*arrick had injured Victoria's feelings. He could tell because he had been attuned to her reactions since she was a child. Her cheeks pinkened from more than the fire, and she bit her lip as her gaze slid away from his.

Victoria had been a complicated, charming girl, equally bold and tenderhearted. The first time he'd found her in his room, he'd assumed she was there to steal his meager belongings. Of course he'd quickly learned how ridiculous the notion was. While not rich in the way of some peers, Sir Hawkins was Midas in Garrick's youthful eyes.

"I was so happy when Father brought you home." The firelight emphasized the long curl of her lashes. "I hated being an only child."

"I was never meant to be your brother. That's not why your father plucked me from the orphanage." He imparted the fact he'd accepted years ago as gently as he could.

"Why did he choose you?"

"I was a big, strong lad with a sharp mind. My mother was a vicar's daughter and made sure I could read and do my sums.

Sir Hawkins wanted to mold and train me into an effective weapon. He succeeded."

She blinked up at him. "I'm sorry."

"There's no need to apologize. The orphanage was harsh, and I had to fight for every scrap. Still, it was better than being forced out onto the streets to eke out a living by pickpocketing or sweeping chimneys. Your father offered me a future and a purpose. I'm not complaining."

"But you sounded so bitter before. Why?"

It was his turn to avoid her gaze, afraid she'd see straight into the heart of him. "Let's see if we can put together a stew."

He was sure she would forget about his feelings once the reality of their situation had a chance to set in. They would be spending the night in a one-room cottage with a single bed. He glanced to the pile of quilts before focusing on the larder.

"Won't whoever lives here be upset if we use his firewood and eat his food?"

"This is a safe house."

"Yes, it feels safe enough. Unless the owner barges in with a pistol."

Garrick laughed and laid potatoes, carrots, and leeks on the table. "No, I mean it's been outfitted for exactly this purpose. Anyone in our network can retreat here if they need to disappear. We pay a local to keep firewood and food stocked just in case."

"Is there any tea in the cupboard?" Victoria riffled through the larder and pulled out a tin with an exultant, "Aha!"

"There might be something even better." Garrick shifted the cupboard aside and retrieved a bottle of brandy from behind it that had come straight from France. A perquisite of the job. He uncorked the bottle and poured a liberal amount into two chipped, unmatched tea cups. Garrick downed his in one swallow. Victoria picked hers up and sipped as if it were boiling-hot tea.

She coughed but smiled at him over the rim. "Mother only allows me a small glass of port after dinner or one flute of champagne at soirees. According to her, liquor muddles your thoughts and leads to poor decisions."

"Your mother is entirely correct, but we can afford a little muddling while I prepare our dinner." By the time he gathered the water needed for their soup and hung the black pot over the fire, Victoria had downed the contents of her cup and poured herself more.

She propped her chin on her hand and pouted. "I could help if I still had my knife. I forgot to retrieve it after you disarmed me."

Garrick cut the vegetables, dropped them into the small black pot, and seasoned it liberally with salt. It would be simple fare without even a loaf of bread. Not what Victoria was used to.

"I must say I do feel much warmer and delightfully muddled." She raised her arms into a stretch and then plucked the remaining pins from her hair. Snow-dampened curls unspooled, and she finger combed them back from her face. "I understand why Mother would be worried if I over imbibed."

Garrick mouth had gone dry. He wasn't sure he could speak even if a pistol were being held to his temple. Watching her perform the mundane task of taking her hair down nearly unmanned him. It was an act only a maid or husband should be privy to, yet here he was with a front-row seat.

He remembered that day they'd been alone in her father's study, the day he'd succumbed to his longing for her. The two years since had blunted the constant frisson of tension between them, but the afternoon at the modiste had awakened his desire like a hibernating bear, starved and ready to devour her. The silence built until it was unbearable.

"How many times have you used this cottage?" she asked.

"Twice."

"Where are we exactly?"

"North of London."

"That's not exactly exact." Her look was so sardonic, he fought a smile and lost.

"The more people who know about this place, the less safe it is."

Her hum was full of annoyance. She took a sip and examined him over the rim of the cup. "Because you never mentioned a life before the orphanage, I assumed you had been abandoned there as a babe, but you weren't."

He shook his head but said nothing, not expecting her to circle back to their earlier conversation.

"What happened?"

"An illness took my mum and da within days of one another. I was ten." He felt like he'd swallowed a whole turnip and it had stuck in his throat.

She slipped her bare fingers around his palm and gave his hand a squeeze. Her skin rasped delicately against his. "I'm so sorry. I should have asked. Why didn't I think to ask?"

He stared at their hands. His large and rough, hers slender and strong. "Because you were young and sheltered and such tragedy would never have occurred to you."

"Tell me about your parents."

He hadn't talked about them for years. At first his grief had been too raw, and later he'd learned missish feelings invited bullying in the orphanage. To cry was the mark of weakness, so he'd buried his grief and love and had never attempted to excavate them. Why bother now?

"They were good people." He shrugged and tried to sound dismissive. "From what I remember."

"What did your father do for a living?"

Her questions were a spade to his defenses. "Blacksmith."

"Ah, you must take after him. You're very…" Her voice

petered into nothing. He raised his brows, waiting. She cleared her throat, and whispered, "Strong."

"Yes, Da was a big man. Mum called him a gentle giant. He would bring home strangers in need of a hot meal." The years had dulled Garrick's memory like a watercolor left in the rain, but his da's laugh was indelible. Even so many years later, hearing a deep, booming laugh would spin Garrick around in search of his long-dead father. "His kindness got him killed."

"But you said he was felled by illness."

"One of his charity cases was sick and died on a cot in the smithy. Mum and Da were taken by the same sickness not two weeks later, a day apart." He didn't like revisiting the memory of his indomitable da gaunt and weak, dying in the same bed his mum had died in the day before.

So much death. It was only when he went to war that he became inured to it.

"You had no relatives to go to? No one in the village offered to take you in?"

"They were afraid of me. Three people had just died in our cottage of some unknown plague. They burned the cottage and the smithy and banished me from town."

"They burned your cottage down and refused to take you in? That's barbaric. Heinous. It makes me want to—" She slammed her fist on the table, jostling the cups.

Her outrage on behalf of the ten-year-old boy he had been resettled something inside of him. He had tried to justify the way men, women, and children who had known him all his life had reacted, but he finally felt entitled to the anger he'd tried to deny. His da had been an important part of the village and had helped everyone at one time or another. Yet the villagers had only offered Garrick their backs.

"What would you do?" he asked.

"I would rain curses upon them. I would visit them in the dead of night and release a wild boar in their houses. I would see them on their knees in the town square begging for your forgiveness." Ruthlessness shrouded her words with an ominous promise.

He smiled in spite of himself. She was her father's daughter. "I understand now," he said.

"Understand what?"

"Why Lady Eleanor came to you for help. You are a protector by nature and a formidable woman. More so than anyone realizes."

The ghost of a smile crossed her lips. "Would you please tell Mother? She seems to think I must marry in haste because I require protection. You've seen the gentlemen who come to call. Tell me the truth. Would any have been able to best the men in the alley and protect me?"

He declined to answer her question and focused on what made his heart pound faster. "Marry in haste?"

"Indeed. Mother wants me to pick a likely candidate at the Stanfields' yuletide house party." A sly smile spread her lips. "Can we hide here together until it's over?"

"I'm afraid we won't be trapped here for long." Garrick turned to stir the soup to hide his reaction at the thought of spending days—and more to the point, *nights*—alone with Victoria. The feeling approached an intense longing. But he longed for the impossible.

"Are you hungry?" he asked.

"Starving."

He doled out the watery soup into two clay bowls, and they set about eating. Her surprise couldn't be contained on her first bite. "This is not nearly as bad as I expected. Where did you learn to cook? From your mother?"

"At the orphanage. All the boys rotated through a set of chores. One week was kitchen duty. One week was caring for the gardens. Another week was spent cleaning and maintaining the house. I'm quite handy." He'd had to be or risk getting beaten.

"You have skills I could never dream of." She shot him a teasing smile, harkening back to their conversation that morning outside Sir Hawkins's study door. It seemed a lifetime ago.

They finished the soup. Garrick cleaned the pot and bowls in the brook and gathered clean water to heat for their ablutions. Flakes drifted like stars from the slice of black sky visible through the treetops. The snow had been a piece of good fortune. Several inches had accumulated to cover their tracks, but the rate was slowing. Was it wrong to wish to be buried in the cottage with Victoria for weeks?

Foolishness is what it was. He was bound to protect her and return her unhurt and untouched to Sir Hawkins.

Victoria was stoking the fire when he returned. There was enough wood to keep them warm until morning. She stood and swayed slightly. Her dress hung like a sack, and he spotted the bundle of padding she had worn underneath across the foot of the bed.

"Go on and lie down while the water heats." He settled himself in one of the stiff-backed wooden chairs and tried not to think about how much more comfortable the bed would be, especially with Victoria in it.

The rustle of clothing sounded, and this time he kept his gaze fixed on the fire. One lapse was one too many.

"Might I beg a favor?" Her voice was soft and hesitant. "Without my maid, I can't quite…"

He mouthed a curse to the gods of temptation and went to her. She presented the column of buttons up her spine and neck. He worked the top button free of its loop. His intention to make quick work of the task was forgotten. His fingers trembled and fumbled with each button.

The unveiling of her graceful neck was slow and sensuous

and utter torture. By the time he reached the top of her shift and the laces of her stays, he was fighting the urge to lay a kiss where her neck and shoulder met.

Onward he worked until all the buttons were finally freed and he was trapped in a fever dream. He'd imagined undressing Victoria many times over the years; he'd just never expected to be in this position and unable to touch her.

"There. All done." He took a step back and clenched his hands behind his back.

"I can't sleep in my stays. Would you mind loosening the laces?" She glanced at him over her shoulder. Her cheeks were flushed, and her blue eyes glittered in the firelight.

He hesitated, gathering his self-control like a shield.

A half smile tipped her lips as she shrugged the bodice off her shoulders. "Come now. You've seen me in less. Much less."

Embarrassment burned through him. He pulled at his collar and wondered if steam was rising off his shoulders. "I'm terribly sorry about this morning. I'm not sure what happened. I should have—"

"Stop!" Her smile vanished, and she glared at him a moment before turning her face away. In a less vehement tone, she continued, "I could have screamed or swooned or simply closed the curtain all the way. I didn't. I harbor no regrets and hope you don't either."

"Victoria." He was at a loss for anything else to say. Neither of them moved.

"Do you ever think about it?" she whispered.

"About what?"

"The kiss."

The kiss. He was an expert liar when his life was in peril, and this moment certainly felt charged with danger. Yet… "Every time I see you. Every bloody day and night."

The telltale movement of her shoulders signaled her

increased rate of breathing. He, on the other hand, was frozen and light-headed from lack of air.

"My stays?" Her voice was remarkably calm, and he didn't speak for fear of betraying how deeply she affected him.

He did his duty, no matter how much it pained him, and loosened her stays, making sure his fingertips didn't stray to her skin. A single touch would be *his* undoing. Without waiting for his retreat or asking him to avert his gaze, Victoria pushed her dress and stays to the floor in one fluid motion and whirled around.

He reeled backward but didn't get far in the tiny cottage. His arse hit the table, and he clutched the edges, grateful for the support when she stepped out of her clothes toward him. Firelight danced off her skin, the thin cotton doing little to conceal her lush form.

He opened his mouth to protest, but only a rumbling groan of surrender emerged.

"I might have died tonight if it weren't for you." She pulled the pink ribbon at the neck of the garment. Excruciatingly slowly, the ribbon unfurled, and the fabric parted.

The shadowy valley between her breasts drew his gaze, and he swallowed. The curves of her breasts were tempting him toward another bout of insanity. Her chemise slipped off one shoulder and sagged low enough for one nipple to peek over.

"I don't expect a reward. Especially not this," he said roughly.

"You don't want me?" Any boldness she projected fell away in a blast of insecurity that had her biting her lip and looking away. "You kissed me in the alley. Why?"

As smart and defiant and reckless as Victoria might be, she was still an innocent with tender feelings. Would it be so terrible to reassure her of her attractions without compromising her?

His conscience mocked the weak justification even as he stepped forward, wrapped his arm around her, and pulled her flush against him. Her nearly naked body molded itself against him like molten metal.

She trailed her hands up his arms to loop around his neck and tipped her head back, her request as clear as an engraved invitation. The moment he'd dreamed about was upon him, but his imagination hadn't done it justice.

He cupped her cheek with one hand, his thumb glancing over her cheekbone, and lowered his mouth to hers, the touch gentle yet packing a punch that stole his breath. Her lips were soft and parted on a sigh.

Time wrinkled, and they were back in her father's study, picking up where they'd left off two years earlier. Except with fewer clothes and complete privacy and one bed beckoning from the corner.

The kiss metamorphized from gentle to wild like the progression of a storm. She grabbed his lapels and shoved his jacket off his shoulders without breaking their connection. He clawed at his sleeves until he was free and tossed his jacket to the floor.

Their tongues danced. The give and take was painfully erotic and evocative in ways that made his cock throb. He firmed his hold around her waist, picked her up, and reversed their positions, setting her on the table.

She let out a breathy exclamation, her nails gripping his shoulders. He worked his hips between her knees and maneuvered her to the edge of the table. She bit her lip and worked her body even closer, until her legs were wrapped around his hips and the thick length of his cock was pressed against the juncture of her thighs.

"So you do want me. Your cock is hard," she said in a husky, playful voice that made him even harder.

A slight laugh huffed out of him. "Where did you hear such language?"

"I've read things. And heard things." Her lashes swept down

before she once again boldly met his eyes. "But I've never actually experienced such things, and I want to. With you."

"You should only be experiencing such things with your husband." Even as he said the words, he rocked his cock against her, cursing the fabric between them. He wanted her naked and laid out on the table for him to devour and fuck.

"Do husbands not experience such things before marriage?"

"That's different."

"Because I'm a woman and you're a man?"

"Because you are a lady, and I am *not* a gentleman. Society might look askance at a lord's bad behavior, but you would be ruined, Victoria. You would be ostracized and hurt. I couldn't bear that."

"I'm already ruined in the eyes of society by being alone with you all night. You can't say you don't want me. Your gaze on me this morning at the modiste said differently, as does your body right now."

Even as his body clamored for satisfaction, he leaned closer and placed his forehead against hers. "You know I want you, Victoria. I have always wanted you."

He more than wanted her. He loved her and had loved her since the day Sir Hawkins had brought him home and she'd greeted him like she'd been waiting for him all her life.

A half sob escaped her throat. She grabbed his nape and kissed him. A kiss of fire and pent-up need. His reaction equaled her intensity but was tempered by the knowledge there was a world outside the cottage that would judge her harshly for giving in to her passions. But could he give her a taste? He could satisfy her even if he was left bereft.

"Love, would you let me...?" He kissed her and ran his hand from her knee up her thigh, tugging the hem of her chemise higher.

Her skin was soft and supple under his callused palm. When his fingertips grazed the soft hair of her mons, she tensed, and he stilled his advance. He broke their kiss and skimmed his lips over her jaw to tug her earlobe between his teeth. She moaned and let her legs relax, welcoming him.

"I can satisfy you without taking your maidenhead." He ran a finger over the silk of her folds. She was wet. So wet, the temptation to unbutton his breeches and release his cock nearly ground his best intentions to dust. She was ready and willing to be filled by him.

She propped her hands behind her and leaned on them. Her chemise rode high on her thighs, giving him a tantalizing glimpse between them. Her chemise drooped under a breast, framing the perfection. Her nipple was dark pink, delicate, and ruched, and it begged for his mouth. She was a picture of wanton desire.

"Thomas." Her husky whisper brought his gaze to hers. "Please."

CHAPTER 6

*V*ictoria wasn't quite sure what she was begging for. Yes, she had read a multitude of inappropriate texts on the subject of male-female relations. Even the anonymous diary of a courtesan that had scandalized society when it was printed in the midst of the season. She didn't consider herself a complete innocent. Yet the need coursing through her made her feel callow and overwhelmed and desperate.

She couldn't even blame the buzzing warmth of the brandy. The food and conversation had blunted any mind muddling it had incited earlier. She was in full control of her faculties. His gaze on her body was heated and intense, his expression taut, emphasizing the harsh planes of his face. What did he see?

She glanced down. Her breath caught, hardly recognizing herself. Her legs were spread, and his hand was between them, his fingers stroking her to the edge of insanity. Her breast was uncovered, her nipple pebbled. She had never been so exposed to another, physically or emotionally.

She drew her hands into fists on the table, fighting the urge to cover herself. Thomas would take care of her. He had always taken care of her. His fingers were thick and agile, his confident touch different from her own shy explorations.

"How will you satisfy me?" The question came from a place of uncertainty on her part, but a sly smile tipped his lips as if he thought her teasing him.

"How would you like me to satisfy you? With my fingers or my mouth?"

She gasped. The courtesan had made mention of a lover giving her a kiss between her legs, but Victoria had assumed it was an uncommon practice. "I didn't know gentlemen gave ladies such treatment."

Thomas's eyebrows rose. "As I've warned you before, I'm no gentleman."

"Perhaps not by birth, but you are a gentleman in every way that counts."

"Our current position would indicate otherwise." He dipped his head and captured her nipple between his lips in a move reminiscent of his nickname, Hawk.

She surrendered. Her eyes fluttered closed, and she let her head fall back. Pleasure spiraled from where his tongue flicked her nipple and collided with the sensations his fingers were evoking between her legs. Never had she felt anything so exquisite. Or overwhelming. Her arms trembled and began to fold, but he swept his arm around her back for support.

He worked alchemy between her legs. He rubbed the most sensitive spot while one of his fingers played at her entrance. It was the best possible torture. If he asked, she would confess all her secrets.

Like how much she loved him, had always loved him, and would always love him.

Instead, he pushed his finger inside her the same time he lightly bit her nipple. Any complex thought was stamped out by a single chant. *More.* She needed more. Wiggling her hips, she attempted to get closer, but he tightened his arm and kept her from driving farther onto his finger.

"Give me more." Her voice was breathless and hoarse, as if she'd spent the evening begging him for mercy.

The noise he made was pained. "I want to, but I can't."

With shallow movements, he pumped his finger in and out of her in a rhythm that she recognized even though it was her first time. She grasped his shoulders, the solidness of him reassuring her. If she fell, he would catch her. Of that she had no doubt. Her legs quivered. He transferred his mouth from her breasts to her lips and kissed her.

She inched closer to the fog-shrouded precipice and the mystery beyond, finally succumbing. Pleasure dizzied her, and she buried her face in his neck. Her body clamped his finger and wished for more. She drifted back to earth like a falling leaf. Exhaustion swamped her in the aftermath.

Thomas fixed the bodice of her chemise, tying the delicate ribbon, and stepped from between her legs to sweep her into his arms. He carried her to the bed and tucked her under the thick quilt.

She could barely keep her eyes open. "I'm sorry," she mumbled.

"For what?"

"For not returning the favor." She grazed a finger down the length of his cock, hard and pressing against the front of his breeches.

He jerked his hips out of reach. "Ah. I didn't expect you to, love."

"It's only fair." Her eyes were leaden, and it would take a herculean effort to open them. Just as she was drifting to sleep, her mind poked her back awake with a detail that felt important. "You called me 'love.' Twice."

"Rest. We don't know what tomorrow might bring."

The questions she wanted to ask—would the men from the alley be looking for them and did he love her—popped like soap bubbles, disappearing entirely as sleep claimed her. A sleep interrupted by the unusual surroundings and the fact she wasn't alone.

She stirred once to see Garrick on his haunches stoking the fire and another to find him looking out the small, grimy window with a predator's stance. Both times, she drifted back into a restless darkness marked by dreams alternately fearful and erotic.

Diffuse morning light brought her to full wakefulness. The fire still crackled and warmed the cottage, but a different kind of heat radiated next to her. She turned her head on the pillow. Garrick was stretched out next to her on top of the quilt, his arms crossed over his chest.

Sleep blunted the angles and edges of his face, and she could see hints of the boy he'd been before tragedy had taken his parents. The suddenness and totality of his loss made her heart ache.

Not only had both his parents died, but he'd lost his home and village and everything familiar. One week he'd been safe and secure in his place in the world, and the next he'd been thrown into an orphanage with no one to love and no one to love him.

She turned on her side and drank him in. His dark hair was thick and wavy and mussed. Her fingers twitched to push a stray lock off his forehead. His sleek eyebrows, blade of a nose, and strong jaw could have been carved on a coin. The curve of his lashes and the surprisingly sensuous fullness of his lower lip softened what was otherwise unrelenting hardness.

He wasn't handsome by ton standards, but he was attractive in a way she couldn't quantify. He had the face of a battle-tested knight. What lady could resist giving him her favor?

Her gaze wandered over the strong column of his throat to where the hard planes of his chest and a peppering of dark hair peeped out of his shirt. His biceps bulged where they crossed over his chest. She stared at his fingers for a long moment, remembering the magic they had wrought. Heat enveloped her, and she pushed the covers to her waist and continued her examination, her head propped on her hand. His stomach was taut, and his... She swallowed at the ridge visible in his breeches. Had he been in such a state since their encounter?

The tightness in her lower belly made her squirm, and her breasts grew heavy and sensitive. The uncomfortable, restless feeling had returned full force, but now she knew he had the ability to appease her need. She didn't want to dwell on how he had acquired such talents.

The confrontation with the two men in the alley had upturned what she'd thought she knew about herself. An unfamiliar vulnerability had shaken her footing. Thomas hadn't taken advantage of her battered confidence or the brandy fuzzing her senses the night before. He could have. She'd certainty begged him to.

The morning brought clarity. A clarity society would deem madness.

She laid a hand on his stomach between his folded arms and the top of his breeches. His breathing remained deep and even, and he didn't so much as twitch a muscle. She glided her hand to the nearest button of his fall and ever so slowly slid it free.

She glanced up, but his face remained impassive. Biting her bottom lip, she slid her hand into the narrow opening. Her fingertips brushed the hard length of him covered in thin cotton. With a startling quickness, Thomas clamped her wrist.

Oh dear. She'd been caught with her hand in the biscuit tin.

"What the devil are you doing?" His voice was raspy with sleep.

"Is it not obvious?"

He turned his head on the pillow, and their gazes collided. He remained on his back. Her hand remained in his breeches.

Their faces were too far away to share a kiss, but close enough she could see the shards of dark amber around his pupils. His expression was a clash of shock and wonder.

With the slowness of a stalking cat, she inched her hand farther inside until the pads of her fingers stroked his length through the cotton. His hand spasmed on her wrist, and his eyes widened with his sharp intake of breath. Yet he didn't protest.

Her own breathing picked up as she curved her fingers over his cock. She explored the thick length of him, from the taut sacs below to the spear-shaped tip. Imagining his cock in place of his finger gave her a moment's pause. Would he fit? Her body had no such qualms. She ached to have him between her legs and could feel herself growing slick with want. This time it wasn't her but him who begged.

"Please." The word emerged on a chesty groan.

"Do you want me to stop?" She tightened her grip, and his cock pulsed in her hand, making her catch her breath.

"Of course I don't, but we can't..." His hips moved restlessly, not away, but into her touch.

"Of course we can." Whether they *should* was a different debate. Actually, any sane person would argue they shouldn't. If they did nothing, at least when their adventure was concluded, she could claim her innocence. Mostly.

It wasn't merely her night in a cottage with Garrick that was an issue. Lord Berkwith had seen her being pulled into an alley with two ruffians. Only his gentlemanly discretion, which was in question to begin with, stood between her and ruination.

Her mother would already have a plan brewing on her return. Victoria would be married off before any rumors sifted through society. She would be another man's wife, expected to share his bed whether she wanted to or not. Fate had given her the opportunity to be with the one man she truly wanted and loved. She'd read enough books to know not to thumb her nose at fate.

"Mother wants me to marry soon. Very soon."

"All the more reason for us to stop this madness." Yet he didn't pull away, giving her a shot of hope that was more potent than the brandy.

"There's only been one man who has ever stirred my blood. Only one man whose bed I've dreamed of sharing."

He squeezed his eyes shut, and his expression could only be described as tortured. Was she winning or losing the argument?

Unable to keep the desperation from her voice, she continued, "I realize you're a man of the world and have experience with this sort of thing. I've only read how to please a man and will probably be a disappointment, but if you could find it in your heart to—"

He jerked the quilt off her and rolled half on top of her in a rush of movement that shocked her into silence. His elbows were braced on either side of her head, his lips an inch from her. "Hush, woman."

He kissed her, slow and languorous, yet with an underlying intensity of being lured into a trap. She was more than happy to be caught.

She relaxed under his weight, enjoying the feel of him. One of his legs was braced between hers, and his erection was pressed against her thigh. Tentatively, she raised her hands from the mattress and lay them lightly along his flanks. His muscular bulk stirred her senses.

"I need to confess something." He spoke the words between drugging kisses.

She hummed before nipping the sensuous curve of his bottom lip between her teeth. He raised himself out of the reach of her mouth, and she pretended to pout, hoping he hadn't changed his mind.

"You mentioned I'm a man of the world with experience."

A blush lit her from head to toe. "I want to please you, if you'll teach me."

Red burnished his cheeks, and his chuckle was self-depreciating. "I have experience with many things, but not as much as you are assuming."

"But last night you knew exactly what to do."

The red from his cheeks traveled down his neck. "I'm not entirely inexperienced, but I've never... bedded a woman."

Thomas was a virile, attractive man. She'd seen the way the maids had eyed him. He'd had countless opportunities. Of that she had no doubt. "Why not?"

His rare smile made a bittersweet longing swell in her chest. "Don't you know?"

"Because of me?" The slight creak in her voice was a sign of her rising emotion.

For years, she'd assumed her feelings for Thomas were unrequited. Their kiss had renewed her infatuation, but two long years had passed without an overture from him. Her dreams had felt out of reach, and if not for this unexpected turn of events, she might never have had him in her grasp.

"Of course because of you."

She swallowed back a lump of tears. Turning into a watering pot might put him off. No, it wouldn't. She smiled through a haze of tears, wrapped her hand around his nape, and pulled him down for a kiss.

"We'll figure it out together. I've read quite a bit more than I should have on the subject. If you would like me to share."

"Yes, I know about your sojourns to the bookshops and what you bought."

"I was wondering why you didn't comment on my attire and the padding." Her forays were well thought out and perfectly executed. Even her parents were none the wiser. "How long have you known?"

"Since the beginning. Your father tasked me with keeping your safe. I made it my business to know what you were up to. Your disguise was quite good, but not good enough to fool me."

"You didn't tell Father."

"Make no mistake, I would have if I thought you were endangering yourself, but I understand how restricting you find your role since your debut. It has pained me to watch your natural curiosity stifled by conventions."

He understood. She didn't need to hide her true self from him. It was like a too-tight set of stays had been loosened. And knowing they were on equal footing in bed made her even bolder.

"Speaking of my natural curiosity." She ran her hands down his back to the hard muscles of his buttocks and dug her fingers in. "You have very much aroused it."

He tugged the ribbon and pulled her chemise off her shoulders, not stopping until her breast were exposed to his gaze. There was nowhere to hide with the morning sun offering illumination, so she didn't try. Instead, she arched her back in invitation.

He accepted with gusto. He lathed her nipple with his tongue before pulling the peak inside his mouth for a hard suck. Pinpricks rushed through her and made her squirm. She pulled his shirt from his breeches and rucked it up his chest, needing him as naked and vulnerable as she was. He grabbed hold of the back and pulled it over his head. She ran her hands up his chest and pushed him away a few inches in order to see what he'd unwrapped.

Before she had the chance to make a thorough examination, he switched their positions in a show of strength that made her weak in the knees. He ended up half sitting against the pillows, with her straddling him, and his cock pressed between her legs. A blush started in her cheeks and couldn't be contained. Pink raced across her breasts.

"Are you embarrassed?" he asked with a quirk of his brows.

"I'm embarrassed and aroused and desperate and scared and about a thousand other things I can't explain."

"Concentrate on the pleasure. The rest we will figure out together."

Yes, together. She took a deep breath. His gaze fixed on her chest, and his hands followed. He cupped her breasts and thrummed her nipples with his thumbs. She pitched forward and braced her hands on his chest. The muscles shifted and dark hair tickled her palms. She forgot about her embarrassment.

She ran her hands over his shoulders and back over the planes of his chest. Multiple scars traced their way over his skin. She hurt to think of him hurt. How close had he come to death?

She touched a recent one with her finger. "What happened here?"

He shifted and looked down at where she pointed. "Got into a fight with a stick while I took cover in a stream."

A disbelieving laugh burst out of her. She had expected a harrowing tale involving stilettos and evil Frenchmen.

"Oh, you laugh, but it hurt like the devil, and I had to keep quiet or risk getting caught." His grin was as close to boyish as she'd ever seen on his face.

She leaned in to kiss his smiling lips. "Whether a stick or a dagger, I never want to see you on the pointy end."

"A sentiment I wholeheartedly agree with. Do you have any scars to discover?" Before she realized what he was about, he had her chemise up and over her head and tossed it on top of his discarded shirt.

She was entirely naked. His face lost any boyishness, and he grew taut everywhere, but most especially between her legs. Her hips rolled in response, and a small moan slipped out. She touched the waist of his breeches. He nodded but didn't make a move to continue her earlier work. She shifted backward and attacked the buttons with shaking hands. Her fumbling only heightened the tension.

Once the fastenings were loosened, Victoria tugged. He

took control, bucking her off and kicking off his breeches. He knelt on the bed, one leg between hers, and pushed her to lie back.

She stared at the appendage jutting from a nest of dark hair between his legs. She'd seen statues of naked men. She'd even seen sketches in the courtesan's diary, but neither had prepared her for the reality. Slowly, as if it were an easily spooked animal, she reached out and touched him.

"Go on," he said in a rumbly voice. "It won't bite."

She shot him a smile and grasped him. He twitched in her hand, and she drew in a quick breath. His cock was hard, but the skin covering him was soft. A slit in the head glistened with fluid, and she explored the spear-shaped tip, running a thumb along the slit and gathering the slippery fluid.

Thomas gripped her thighs and pushed them apart. He stared between her legs with the same fascination she felt regarding his cock. Like the previous evening, he stroked and toyed with her until she was squirming with urgency.

She surrendered even as she mounted a weak protest. "Wait. You're supposed to enter me."

"I will, but this will make things easier for you." His voice was strained. "I hope."

The ominous qualifier barely registered before her climax took hold. This time his fingers drove deep within her, pumping hard through her bliss, extending it. His fingers retreated, and she raised her head to complain, but he had shifted to kneel between her legs.

He gripped his shaft and rubbed the head of his cock through her wetness until he was pressed at her entrance. "Are you ready?"

"Yes. And very willing," she answered breathlessly.

He pushed inside of her, one slow inch at a time. A sheen of sweat broke over his brow. "Am I hurting you?" he asked between clenched teeth.

"No." She was lying. Her body burned as it stretched to accommodate his length and girth.

He pushed until his hips were seated against hers, pinning her legs wide. "It will get easier."

"How do you know?" She bit her lip.

His laugh edged closer to a groan. "I don't. Do you want me to stop?"

She actually considered his question, but as the seconds ticked off, she found the pain subsiding into a different sort of ache. "No, don't stop. What's next?"

"Next, I do this." He withdrew almost all the way, then pressed into her again. Sensation jolted through her when his hips met her body.

"That was... Do it again."

He did. And again and again and again until she lost count. The slide of him in and out of her had become easier, and the friction felt rather magnificent.

"I can't... You feel too good." He withdrew and pumped himself. Fluid spurted onto her belly, warm and copious. Breathing hard, he collapsed at her side.

Neither of them moved for a long moment. Victoria touched the cooling fluid. It smelled earthy and foreign. She brought her finger to her lips and tasted him. Salty and primal. She hummed.

Garrick was watching her with hooded eyes. "You're trying to kill me, aren't you?"

"I was curious."

He leaned over her and kissed her. A long, slow, drugging kiss. He broke away only long enough to retrieve a square of rough linen to wipe her belly clean. "I love your curiosity."

He moved over her again, and for a moment, she thought they were going to do it all over again, but he slid down her body, laying kisses along his path. "I need to apologize though."

"W-why?" She tried to close her legs, but his broad shoulders were in the way.

He lay a kiss above her mons. "I hurt you, and you did not reach your climax with me."

"You only hurt me for a moment, and I climaxed before. And last night." His head dipped, and he flicked his tongue over her still slick folds. She made a sound of surprise when he wiggled his tongue over a sensitive bud. "On the other hand, I shall not complain if you would like to make amends."

His humming chuckle was nearly her undoing. She spread her legs wider and tilted her hips, all modesty at their position forgotten. He worked the bud with his tongue and lips while he gently stroked her folds.

Her climax hit her fast and hard, and she cried out his name while fisting his hair. *Le petit mort.* The little death. Except she felt more alive than she ever had. Her limbs were heavy and replete with pleasure. The aftermath was hazy, but she was aware of him kissing his way up her body to reach her mouth. His taste was indescribable, and she realized she was on his tongue and lips.

How could she ever share her bed with another?

CHAPTER 7

*G*arrick was in heaven. Or as close to heaven as he was likely to come. The woman of his dreams was naked in his arms. Victoria's head was cushioned on his shoulder, and her leg was draped over his. Her curls tickled his chin.

His body was still tingling from the aftermath of their lovemaking. He'd never expected the act to be peppered with laughter and soul-exposing kisses and confessions. Had he said too much or not enough? What would happen when they left the cottage?

Stomach-turning worry loosened the grip of his sensual haze. He needed to check on his horse and determine their next steps. Assuming Garrick's message had reached Sir Hawkins, his mentor would have left word for him through their usual channel.

He'd stayed awake a good part of the night, alert for signs anyone had tracked them, but neither horse nor man had disturbed the falling snow. He sat up and swung his legs out of bed. The banked fire kept the cold at bay, but he flipped the quilt over Victoria to keep her warm.

She ran her hand down his back. A shiver of pleasure

cascaded through him, and his semihard cock let its wishes be known. Given very little encouragement, he could take her again.

"You're beautifully formed, Thomas."

He smiled over his shoulder. The quilt was wrapped around her torso, leaving her arms and shoulders bare. Her dark curls tumbled over the pillow. Never had he dared to dream he would see her like this. The intimacy took his breath away.

"I could say the same and more about you, love." Emotion he tried to stifle hoarsened his voice.

The same questions he struggled with reflected back at him in her eyes, but as he had no answers to offer, he rose and pulled on his clothes, turning his attention to the practical matter of staying alive.

"I'm going to check on my horse. The kettle is full of water if you want to warm it to freshen yourself or boil it for tea. There might even be some sugar stashed in the cupboard." He shot her a glance from the door and ducked into the cold winter world. His horse was content in the lean-to under a woolen blanket. After letting him feed and drink, Garrick saddled him. It was likely to be another long ride.

Garrick walked the perimeter of the meadow, but nothing had disturbed the snow except the light prints of a fox. With an armful of wood, Garrick reentered the cottage, half hoping Victoria was still lounging under the covers naked and would invite him to join her.

She was up and dressed, minus the fastenings she couldn't reach, and rummaging through the cupboard, muttering to herself. The dark braid of her hair swung over her shoulder, tendrils escaping like curling vines.

"Aha!" She emerged with a swipe of dust along her cheek holding a tin. She checked inside and smiled, her eyes sparkling. "The sugar is a bit clumpy, but clumpy sugar is better than no sugar at all in my estimation."

She was remarkedly unfazed by their situation and what had transpired the past twelve hours. He cradled the wood, not sure what to do or say in the circumstances. Should he apologize? Assure her they would be fine? She seemed to require neither.

"Whatever is the matter?" Her eyes flared. "Did you see evidence the men followed us?"

"No," he croaked out. "I fear I've taken advantage of you."

She slammed the sugar tin on the table and propped her hands on her hips. Without the added bulk around her middle, the dress hung loosely. "If you would like to distribute blame, then I must bear the majority. After all, it was my hand in your breeches, was it not?"

"You harbor no regrets?"

Without answering, she took the wood from his arms one log at a time and stacked it by the hearth. Then she stepped into his chest and wrapped her arms around him. "None whatsoever. Do you?"

He lay his cheek on top of her head. "Only as it pertains to the future."

"Are you worried about what Father will say?"

He jerked back to look her in the eyes. "What he will say? He can never know about our… indiscretion."

Her eyes turned as hot as the blue part of a flame and singed him. If that wasn't indication enough that he'd said the wrong thing, her icy tone confirmed his idiocy. "What was I thinking? Of course he will never know about this indiscretion. This was merely a hump. A screw. We swived. It was a way to pass the time that was a bit more satisfying than a game of hazard."

She dropped to her haunches and stoked the fire with the poker. Sparks erupted and snow sizzled. Steam was rising from the black kettle hanging over the fire.

Part of him wanted to laugh at the ridiculousness of her diatribe and ask where she'd learned such words, but her feelings were too raw for teasing. When she rose, he took her arms, but she stared at the middle of his chest. Was she attempting to eviscerate his heart with her gaze?

"Your parents want you to marry a gentleman of means. Someone who can take care of you."

"You take care of me." It felt like an accusation.

He clenched his jaw. Didn't she know if he could, he would present himself to Sir Hawkins and offer his hand in marriage? But that was the problem. Marriage was all he could offer. He had no grand house or servants. His profession was dangerous and unpredictable.

"Yes, I can fend off men who would do you harm, but I can't buy you frocks at the best modiste in London. I can't furnish you with a lady's maid. I don't know if I could even afford your book habit."

She waved a hand. "None of that is important."

He caught her hand and brought it to his chest. "It is, Victoria. You don't know because you've never experienced hunger or poverty or privations. I have, and it only takes a week, a day, an hour to be cast out with nothing."

She curled her fingers around his hand and shook her head, her mouth tight. "Happiness must be worth something, and you care about me, don't you?"

"I would not have you cast out of your parents' house and society. You would come to hate me for it, and I couldn't bear it. That is why what has happened here must stay a secret between us. But know this, I will forever hold the memory close to my heart."

The moment of her capitulation reflected in the slump of her shoulders and the shimmer of tears in her eyes before she looked toward the fire. Even though it was for the best and what had to happen, it still hurt. It was not the pain of a punch that would fade, but the ache of a wound that would fester and never heal.

"What will we do now?" she asked in a small voice bereft of

her usual bravado. He hated that he had stripped her of any of her confidence.

"We will have our tea and then head to the village. There we will seek news and sustenance and decide our next move."

In silence, they drank the bitter tea from chipped earthenware mugs. The sugar added a slight sweetness but also an unpleasant grit. Victoria didn't complain.

"May I suggest you reassemble your disguise?"

She gave a sharp nod, tied the padding around her waist and hips, then presented her back so Garrick could help tighten her stays and fasten the sturdy, plain dress. He was careful to make minimal contact with her skin, afraid he would be too weak to resist laying kisses along the path he covered. By the time he finished, his fingers trembled like a drunkard denied blue ruin.

They put the cottage to rights for the next man or woman who might seek haven there. Cloak pulled close around him, he stepped into the snow. Victoria hesitated in the doorway. She was likely to end up cold and damp before the day was done, but there was no reason for her to start with sodden hems.

"May I?" He held out his arms.

"Do I have a choice?"

"You always have a choice."

She rolled her eyes, signaling the return of a portion of her spirit, and harrumphed. "A Banbury tale if I ever heard one. Women have limited choices, and ladies even fewer."

She gestured him closer, and he swept her into a cradle hold. Her hurt had turned to anger. He preferred her spitting fire. His shoulders relaxed despite the burden he carried—both physical and metaphorical. He trudged through the snow toward his horse.

"Someday you'll thank me," he murmured.

She bucked in his arms. The movement caught him off guard, and he half dropped her, thankfully not headfirst, into the snow. "I will never thank you for being a coldhearted arse."

Anger was one thing. What radiated off Victoria was pure fury.

Garrick was not sure what to say, so he said nothing. If her jerky movements as she mounted behind him were any indication, he had chosen poorly, but any explanation he bumbled through now was bound to make things worse.

They plodded toward the village. Garrick tried not to focus on the simmering, silent woman sitting close behind him. Danger stalked them. His job was to protect Victoria, not to offer something she couldn't accept and he couldn't afford. Like his heart.

The woods were silent, their horse's hoof falls muffled. They cleared the tree line, and the village of Upton Heath came into view. It boasted a blacksmith, a baker, and a large common house with an inn. It was on a well-traveled thoroughfare and was a common post for changing horses for the coaches. It reminded him painfully of the small village he had grown up in.

His destination was the baker. The man also responsible for maintaining the cottage. He dismounted and helped Victoria down, running a critical eye over her. The dowdy dress and padding were in place and offered some camouflage, but without the veiled hat, she was pretty enough to draw notice. Her cheeks were rosy from the cold, and curly wisps of hair framed her face. They couldn't tarry longer than necessary else someone was sure to note her passing.

"I'm sure the inn offers a suitable breakfast and perhaps even passable coffee." She looked longingly in that direction.

"I'm sure it does." He ducked into the baker's and took a deep breath.

The baker's wife in his childhood village used to hand out overdone buns and bread from the back door to the village children. He remembered tearing off the burnt edges and devouring the still-warm treats before running off to play. His heart crimped.

The baker emerged from a back room. His apron and hands were dusted with flour, and his face flushed with the heat from the ovens. "What can I do for you and your missus, sir?"

"A loaf of white and two sticky buns," Garrick said. The man nodded, but before he turned away, Garrick added. "London is harsh this time of year, is it not?"

The innocuous comment wiped the smile from the baker's face. Without replying, he disappeared into the back room. When he returned, the bread and buns were wrapped in paper. Garrick pressed coins into the baker's palm. The man didn't bother to count them, only slipped them into a pocket on his apron.

"Anything else, sir?"

"Nothing. Thank you for your service." Garrick and the man exchanged a nod on Garrick's way out the door.

"Let's find out how passable the coffee is." He led them to the inn. The common room was warm and smoky and welcoming. Even better, the coffee was better than passable. The strong, hot brew sharpened his senses.

Garrick passed Victoria a sticky bun while he bit into his. It was delicious. Smoothing the wrapping, Garrick ran a practiced eye over the message written in tiny coded letters along the side. It wasn't a difficult cipher. Garrick crumpled the paper and tossed it into the flames, watching it flare.

Something didn't feel right. He had expected to come across evidence of men tracking them, but even on their headlong rush through London to the cottage, he hadn't sensed anyone following them.

"Your father received my warning but found nothing amiss at the London residence. As a precaution, your parents have set off for the house party a day early, and I'm to deliver you to them at Danbury. From there, you will travel to the Barclay's manor with no one the wiser." He took a sip of coffee and looked at her over the rim of his cup.

"No one the wiser to the attack or the fact we engaged in carnal relations?"

He sputtered on a swallow, the coffee burning his lungs.

She smiled sweetly before taking a bite of her roll. A dollop of glaze was at the corner of her mouth, and she swiped her tongue over the bit of sweetness. His knees felt unsteady even though he was sitting.

"You mustn't say such things," he whispered.

"Pardon me. I forgot we were ignoring it ever happened."

Her needling worked to make him feel even worse. "You understand why it must remain our secret."

She popped the last bite of sticky bun into her mouth and stared him down for what felt like an eternity. "Of course. Our secret."

"I'm going to see about transportation." He stood and made his escape.

The cold air was a slap in the face. He had ruined everything. Things would never be the same between them. She would become another man's wife, and he would be forced to watch it unfold from outside Sir Hawkins's study door. His life would be a living hell. A sickly combination of anger and despair churned his stomach.

One thing became clear. He must leave Sir Hawkins's employ. With Sir Hawkins's backing and the coin he'd saved, Garrick could buy a commission and become an officer on the front lines instead of a shadowy figure behind the machinations. The simplicity of charging into battle to kill or be killed held its attractions.

After shaking himself out of his stupor, he spoke with the stable master. The sun was bright overhead, and the sound of melting snow dripping from eaves was all around them. The yard had turned into a slushy, muddy mess. According to the stable master, the roads were worse, and progress would be slow in a coach.

Garrick didn't want to remain in the village any longer than necessary, and traveling in a slow-moving carriage would make them easy targets. The only option was to proceed on horseback. Luckily, Victoria was an experienced rider. The weather would make the journey miserable, but she had borne worse with little complaint.

While the stable master readied a sturdy mare for hire, Garrick returned to collect Victoria. Lost in thought and unaware of his approach, she stared into the flames of the hearth, her profile solemn.

The urge to draw her into a comforting embrace made his muscles twitch. Instead, he cleared his throat. "The snow is melting, albeit slowly."

"What is the condition of the road?" She didn't favor him with a glance.

"A combination of mud and slush. Coach travel will be difficult. We'll have to continue on horseback. A mare is being saddled for you now."

She nodded. "I've been thinking."

He braced himself. "About us?"

Now she turned the full force of her attention on him, sitting back in the chair and crossing her arms over her chest. "As a matter of fact, no. About the men who tried to take me."

Garrick took the seat next to her. "What are your thoughts?"

She narrowed her eyes. "Are you only pretending to be interested in what I think to placate me?"

"You are your father's daughter. I don't underestimate the quickness of your mind, and I'm interested in everything you have to say."

She blinked rapidly then let her hands fall to her lap. "You must quit saying such things. It only makes it more difficult."

"Why? It's the truth."

"Because no other man of my acquaintance—not even Father—cares about what I want and even less about what I think." She sighed. "But I will lament over that when I have the luxury of time for a good cry. Right now we must concentrate on why those men wanted to abduct me."

"To get to your father."

"To blackmail him into doing something against the Crown's interest?"

"That would be a solid assumption."

"But how did those men know I would be leaving the town house yesterday evening? Alone. I only decided on a plan of action that afternoon after I visited Eleanor."

"I assume you went through the mews to visit Lady Eleanor as I didn't see you." At her nod, he asked, "Who crossed your path, even if it was for a moment?"

"A groomsman. Annie accompanied me of course."

"Of course she was involved," he said dryly. "I assume you trust her implicitly?"

"I do, and so do you, or she wouldn't be employed in our household."

While Victoria was correct, anyone could be turned if offered the right incentive. "Does she have a suitor? Perhaps a handsome footman placed in a nearby household swayed her with pretty words and cajoled information without her even realizing she was betraying you."

"Is that what you are trained to do? Cajole women out of their secrets?" The jab was well-placed, with the force of enough truth to sting.

"What prompted your hastened visit to Lady Eleanor?" he asked.

"A note from Lord Berkwith passed to me through the milliner."

"Why her?"

"It was at Lord Berkwith's recommendation. A lady visiting the milliner raises few suspicions. I was most often the go-between because I am afforded far more freedom than Eleanor."

"That's because even in your schemes, you exhibit a certain amount of care. Usually."

"I was careful this time. I went well disguised."

"Not careful enough."

"So it seems." She ran a finger along her lower lip, and he followed the path with his gaze, wishing he could lean in and do the same with his tongue. Then he'd—

She whipped around and caught him staring at her mouth. He averted his eyes and picked at the dirt along his cuffs as if he actually cared.

"What does Father preach?" she asked finally.

"Never leave a man alive who can recognize you?"

She sputtered unintelligible words before saying in a shocked whisper, "I've never heard him say such a thing."

He leaned back and crossed his arms. "I think our lessons might have covered different topics. What wisdom did your father impart to you?"

"Don't assume anything."

Garrick had heard Hawkins utter the words so many times they hardly registered anymore, but now he applied them to their situation.

"All right, let's toss the assumption the attempted abduction has anything to do with your father. Do you have enemies? A gentleman scorned? A lady jealous?"

She barked a laugh. "None that I know of. I'm not lofty enough to gain such notoriety nor pretty enough to attract notice from anyone of import."

"Balderdash. You are beautiful and intelligent and any man who isn't besotted with you is an idiot." He took one of her hands in both of his and caressed the back with his thumbs.

It was exactly the sort of gesture he should be avoiding, because it made him want to touch her everywhere. He dropped her hand and rubbed his palms down the legs of his breeches, as if he would ever be able to erase the feel of her skin on his. His little speech was not helping him lock his heart away. He was basically gift wrapping it and offering it on one knee.

"Or maybe not," he said mulishly.

She raised her eyebrows. "Maybe they aren't idiots? Or maybe I'm not beautiful and intelligent?"

An apology stumbled out of his mouth, but when his gaze met hers, her eyes were twinkling with a teasing merriment that was dearly familiar. Some of his dread dissipated. Their second moment of insanity—perhaps hour of insanity was more accurate—hadn't destroyed their friendship.

Garrick didn't have many boon companions. *Any* boon companions. The men and women who worked under Hawkins were chess pieces, never fully realized as people. Garrick was as unknowable to them. He was merely Hawkins's shadow.

To trust was to commit a sin. Nonetheless, Garrick trusted Victoria. Yet another sin he'd committed with her.

"If you have no enemies, it brings us back around to our original theory."

"Not quite." She tapped her forefinger on her lips. "It was, after all, Eleanor who was supposed to be there. However, the likeliest suspect in her abduction would be Lord Berkwith, and he was incapacitated by the men."

"Unless he wanted to make it look like he hadn't hired them."

"But why would it matter at that point? If Eleanor had made an appearance, his assumption would be that she was willing to elope."

"Except she wasn't, was she? If you hadn't taken her place, she was planning to deny him, correct?"

"I suppose, although I believe he could have swayed her to accept him." She shook her head. "What a tangle."

"We can work on unraveling it while we travel. Are you ready?" He rose and tugged on his gloves, considering her. He took his hat and dropped it on her head. "Wear this. I will be cannon fodder if I return you to your mother sunburned."

They ducked into the cold sunshine. The mare was waiting next to a mounting block. Victoria adjusted the bulk of her padding and hauled herself into the sidesaddle. Their horses trudged along the muddy lane. The winds were calm under the sunny skies, and while it was cold, it wasn't brutally uncomfortable. He attuned himself to their surroundings, but nothing seemed amiss.

"What's the matter?" she asked.

"Nothing. No one has followed us that I can tell." He shifted toward her in the saddle. "Doesn't that strike you as odd?"

"You don't have faith in your ability to evade miscreants?" She shot him a small smile. "Could it be we are assigning motives where there are none? What if the men were merely opportunists and unaware of my identity? Not so farfetched a coincidence, considering the area of London."

Garrick harrumphed. He didn't believe in coincidence. One did not abduct Sir Hawkins's only child without an eye to the consequences. The entire might of the British underground network would be brought to heel in order to locate her, and no quarter would be given. The risk was great. What reward had they hoped to gain?

Would Sir Hawkins betray his country and honor to save his daughter? Garrick had seen him sacrifice others without a moment's remorse, and he thanked the gods Sir Hawkins hadn't been tested.

The journey passed pleasantly enough. They discussed favorite foods and theater productions.

"I didn't know you enjoyed the theater." Victoria's smile was one of surprised delight.

"I attend matinees on the odd afternoon with the rest of the rabble."

"So do I!" Her huff dimmed her surprise. "You follow me on my trips to the theater."

While it was a statement, he answered, "I do, but only as a

safeguard. I've come to enjoy the outings as much as you. There were many times I had to stop myself from discussing the productions with you."

"I'm not sure how to feel. Grateful or resentful." The squelch of mud under hooves filled her pondering silence. Finally, she said, "We could have gone together. So much wasted time."

Her conclusion startled him. He'd assumed her resentment revolved around his encroaching on her independence. If he dwelled on their squandered time, he might go around the bend. Instead, he kept his voice light. "Tell me about the books you enjoy."

Victoria told him about the books she'd been reading, and he told her about funny things that had happened to him in service for her father. He didn't talk about the bad, not because she wouldn't understand but because he feared she would offer him comfort he would be hard-pressed to deny.

Dusk was falling when the edge of Danbury came into view. Larger than Upton Heath, it would be easy enough for Victoria to arrive unnoticed and join her parents.

When the inn came into view, Garrick nudged his chin. "You go on. I'll keep watch over you from here. If you need me, I'll come."

Their gazes melded for one long, agonizing moment. "I'll always need you, Thomas."

She nudged her horse forward, dragging his beleaguered heart behind her.

CHAPTER 8

*R*iding away from Thomas sundered her heart. It was the end of a chapter. A cliffhanger, at that. Victoria had no clue what came next. Was it to be a farce, a tragedy, or a romance?

Victoria stepped into the inn. Her mother and father were in heated conversation at the bottom of the stairs leading up to the rooms. With a tight mouth, her mother glanced toward the door, and Victoria was met by a blank face.

Dear Lord, Victoria had forgotten about the extra padding and horrendous dress. Perhaps it would be best if she didn't take off Thomas's hat. She stepped forward and cleared her throat. Her mother's eyes widened, and she said something that had her father whirling around. He took her in head to toe. The corners of his mouth quirked as he approached her.

The almost smile was shocking enough. The kiss he laid on her cheek was absolutely astonishing. "I should have known," he murmured before slipping out of the door, presumably to discuss matters with Thomas.

What should he have known? Could he see the imprint of

Garrick hands and mouth and...? Her cheeks heated and banished the chill of the ride.

Her mother whisked her up the stairs and into a cozy, well-appointed room decorated in blue brocade. A stand with a white-and-blue porcelain basin and pitcher stood next to a bed piled high with blankets. A fire had been laid, and an emerald-green velvet chair stood in the corner.

"What on earth are you wearing?" Her mother's first question a surprise.

Victoria had expected an interrogation about her almost kidnapping and her night alone with Thomas. Or even inquiries about her emotional and physical well-being. Not curiosity about her attire.

"A dress." Victoria tossed Thomas's hat on the bed. She wasn't usually so recalcitrant, but the past twenty-four hours had been life changing. Except, she wasn't sure anything would actually change in her life. Her mother would still expect her to pick a husband at the house party.

"I have been too lenient with you." Her mother's tone took on a glacial edge. "You've been allowed too much independence. I'm afraid it's ruined you."

Although her mother didn't mean ruination by fornication, a weary laugh popped out of Victoria.

"This is no laughing matter. We must hope Lady Eleanor and Lord Berkwith stay silent on your scandalous behavior."

"Considering they would be implicating themselves if they speak of it, I'm sure they will remain quiet. Anyway, Eleanor is my friend."

"A friend would not have allowed you to meet with a man unescorted and unprotected." Her mother's severity quashed any humor Victoria felt. "If whispers of your indiscretion turn into shouts, you won't have a choice but to marry Lord Berkwith, and none of us want that."

Revulsion turned Victoria's insides to mush. For one thing,

she had no interest in a popinjay like Lord Berkwith. Even worse though, was the fact Eleanor fancied herself in love with him, and Victoria wedding him would be the ultimate betrayal.

"How is Eleanor? Did you speak with her?"

"She was nearly hysterical and took to her bed, but the Stanfields are still planning to attend the house party." She harrumphed. "Unless they have locked Lady Eleanor away."

"Perhaps Lord Berkwith will offer for Eleanor." The earnestness in the lord's eyes had swayed her opinion of him, but did he truly love Eleanor? Or was she simply a pretty, pliable, suitable lady with a very attractive dowry?

"Men like Berkwith only care about what someone can do for them. Eleanor is a sweet girl. She deserves better than to be saddled with a man like him." It was perhaps the most honest conversation Victoria had ever had with her mother about the nature of love and marriage.

"Why did you marry Father?" The question popped out, and by the way her mother's eyebrows rose, it surprised them both.

"From the moment I met your father, I recognized his intelligence and ambition. I was ambitious too." Something similar to her father's rock-hard fortitude shimmered in her mother like the reflection on a lake. Perhaps they weren't as ill-suited as Victoria had assumed.

Victoria had never considered her mother ambitious, but she supposed it depended on one's viewpoint. Her mother had been the daughter of a country squire. Now she was the wife of a man who had earned a knighthood and was welcomed along the edges of society. If Victoria made a good marriage, the Hawkins family might be accepted into the heart of the ton.

"You will bathe, change into something appropriate, and then join us for dinner. Lord and Lady Tilbury are also staying here on their way to the Barclays." Her mother's tone turned speculative. "As is their son Lord Percival. A second son, but with prospects. Your presence—smiling and charming—will go a long way to quash any talk. If anyone inquires, you traveled from London with us and have been resting in your room."

"Of course, Mother." Victoria didn't have to force an agreeable tone. Considering the alternative was a possible marriage to Lord Berkwith, she would play her part to dispel any talk. It seemed Lord Percival had emerged as a dark horse for her hand. How could she hobble his chances?

Her mother swept out of the room, and Victoria only had time to remove the padding under her dress before her mother's maid, Margery, appeared. Not five minutes later, a knock on the door signaled the arrival of a shallow tub and pitchers of steaming water.

Her bath was perfunctory, even though she wanted to revel in the warmth and ease her soreness. The long hours of riding, plus her morning activities with Thomas, had left her aching in all sorts of places. She dressed in a long-sleeved gown of dark blue with golden accents around the modest neckline and matching gold braiding around the cuffs and hem.

Margery pinned Victoria's hair up, her frustration with the escaping curls manifesting itself in a rough jab with the final pin. Victoria stared at her reflection. How odd that she didn't look any different when everything had changed.

"Your mother will be waiting." Margery bustled out without a backward glance.

Victoria didn't move for a long moment, wishing the girl in the wavery looking glass could offer a nugget of wisdom. She was at a tipping point. One direction would send her into a safe, albeit unhappy, marriage with a virtual stranger. The other direction was shrouded. That future could well be a disaster, but hope lurked. Could she abandon the faint hope of true happiness for comfort and acceptance?

She didn't have the strength to untangle her feelings tonight. Tonight she would paste on a smile and pretend nothing had changed. Her determination was challenged the moment she entered the private dining room of the inn.

Thomas had tucked himself into a corner and surveyed the scene like his nickname, the Hawk. He had bathed as well, and his dark hair was still damp. She was staring, yet she couldn't stop herself.

She knew what his hands felt like on her skin, knew what he tasted like, knew the pleasure of having him between her legs, and she wanted more. She wanted to wake up next to him every morning and discuss politics and science and art while threading her fingers through his hair.

She almost threw her head back and laughed like a mad woman. Untangling her feelings proved to be simple once she'd cast aside her fears. She loved Thomas Garrick and would happily sacrifice a life as some lord's wife to be with him.

Would he be willing to step into the unknown at her side? No, not completely unknown. The future would be riddled with challenges. Thomas would lose his position for betraying her father's trust. She had been focused on the risks she would incur by wanting Thomas, but he would lose far more. What if he didn't consider her worth the risk? The thought soured her appetite.

"Victoria." Her mother snapped her name.

Victoria gathered herself. The gentlemen were standing and waiting for her to take her seat between her mother and Lord Percival. His father, the Viscount of Tilbury, was at the head, and Sir Hawkins and the viscountess were across the table.

"I'm so pleased our travel plans coincided," Victoria murmured while taking her seat and forcing a smile.

Thomas was behind her and her nape heated. His big hand had grasped her there and guided their lips together. Was he recalling the same moment?

Her father was watching her closely. Of course he watched everything closely. It was why he excelled at subterfuge. A glass of wine was placed in front of her. Victoria glanced at her mother, who nodded. Perhaps her mother understood Victoria needed help to loosen her tongue.

She drained half the glass before taking a bite of food. The warmth settled in her belly. While she wasn't relaxed, she found herself answering questions and making small talk with Lord Percival, even though she couldn't remember a blink later what they had discussed.

Finally, dinner ended. As everyone would rise early to travel to the Barclay's manor house, the party broke up and retired to their rooms, eschewing after-dinner port or any gossiping among the ladies. Lord Percival fell into step alongside Victoria.

"I enjoyed our dinner conversation immensely, Miss Hawkins." Lord Percival was a nice-enough-looking fellow, if a bit spindly and sallow-faced.

"As did I." She prayed he wouldn't quiz her on her favorite topic.

Shooting her a shy smile, he took her hand and pressed a light kiss on the back. "I hope to further our acquaintance at the house party."

"That would be very pleasant, my lord." She retrieved her hand from his grasp and didn't linger.

Her father waited in the hallway outside of her room. "I would speak with you a moment."

Dread tied her stomach into a knot. "Of course, Father."

Was he going to ask her if Thomas had acted inappropriately? Or would he know that she was the one who had instigated their encounter? Would she lie to keep their secret or tell the truth? She lowered herself into the velvet chair, which she realized immediately was a mistake. Even though he wasn't a large man, his presence filled the room as he paced.

"I have been unable to locate the men who attempted to abduct you. What can you tell me?"

"There were two men. Big. Rough."

"How were they dressed? What did they smell like?"

She blinked at the questions, then closed her eyes. "Woolen jackets. One dark blue, the other brown. Unpatched, but worn heavily around the elbows. The man who grabbed me smelled like..." She took a breath through her nose, searching for the scent in her memories. "Onions? Ale?"

Her father hummed thoughtfully, and when Victoria opened her eyes, he loomed over her, pulling at his chin. "What about their accents?"

"They did not speak." She let her father stew over her answers for a moment. "Any theories?"

"While threats against you and your mother have always simmered, the group I suspected was behind the plot doesn't appear to be guilty. That doesn't mean they are innocent though. I shall keep digging until I discover the truth." He sighed and fixed her with his unflinching gaze. It could intimidate even her. Heat prickled her face and chest. "Your mother seems to think you've avoided ruination."

Victoria managed to make a sound that landed near acknowledgment, if not a full-throated agreement.

"I suppose we'll see." He raised a brow as if inviting confessions.

"I suppose we will." The truth burned a hole in her heart, but she said nothing more.

His eyes narrowed. "I'm posting Garrick outside your door tonight."

She popped out of the chair. Having Thomas outside her door was a temptation she would never be able to resist. "He's exhausted, Father. It was a long night and day. Let him rest."

"He's the only man I trust you with, Victoria." He touched her cheek. Her breath stalled. Her father wasn't given to gestures of affection, and he had bestowed two in a matter of hours.

As soon as he stepped out the door, her mother's maid took

his place to help her into her night rail and to stoke the fire. "Is there anything else you require, miss?"

"Nothing. Thank you, Margery."

Despite the chill in the air, Victoria didn't retreat to the bed. She chafed her arms and paced in front of the hearth. She should be exhausted, yet a restless energy zinged through her blood, making her heart pound faster. She wasn't sure what she was waiting for until a rustle sounded in the hall.

Before common sense could override the impulse, she opened the door, grabbed Thomas by the sleeve, and pulled him into the room. She leaned against the closed door, blocking his escape. He had lost his collar and cravat, and his white shirt gaped open at the neck, revealing a tantalizing dusting of dark hair.

Neither of them spoke. They merely stared at one another. Unlike at dinner, his gaze was unflinching and heated. She shivered, but not from cold.

"I shouldn't be here." He kept his voice at a whisper.

"I know," she whispered back. Her father could conceivably check to make sure Thomas was outside her door, but why would he? He trusted Thomas implicitly.

"Lord Percival seems quite taken with you." Was his tone edged in green?

"I don't care a jot about him."

"Will that matter to your mother?"

An ever-growing panic gripped her throat and squeezed. He was right, of course. Her mother was determined she would marry well, and while Thomas might be the best man, he did not qualify as a gentleman in her mother's estimation.

Yet something in his tone gave her hope. If his aim was to put their mistake behind them so Victoria could secure an advantageous future, why would he bring Sir Percival up? "Does it matter to you whom I marry?"

"It shouldn't." Bitterness coated his words.

"Yet it does." The lilt in her voice quavered the words between a statement and a question. The ground they tread was unsteady and dangerous, and she needed him to reassure her.

"Dammit, Victoria." He looked... stricken. "You know it does. I can't bear the thought of you in another man's arms."

She closed the distance between them and wrapped her arms around him. After a blink of time that lasted an eternity, he pulled her tightly against him, running his hands up and down her back, from her buttocks to thread into her hair, tugging it free of the loose braid to tumble around her shoulders.

"This is madness. Sir Hawkins—"

"Doesn't matter. Only we do."

Thomas's chest inflated with a huge breath as if he was preparing an argument, but instead, he buried his face in her neck. Her skin was primed for his touch. His lips sent shivers through her, and she closed her eyes. Her nipples tightened.

"If only that were true. This is impossible... impossible," he murmured.

She felt his words as much as heard them. Yet he didn't push her away. When he moved, he shifted her across the floor with him. She prayed the bed was their destination. It wasn't. He sat in the velvet chair and drew her down with him, positioning her across his lap.

He stroked her hair and held her tightly. She felt too much like a child being comforted after not getting what she wanted. Unacceptable. She pushed off his chest. Any frustration with him vanished. Exhaustion bruised his eyes and sadness blunted his features.

She scrambled around until she straddled him and then took his face between her hands. His night whiskers tickled her palms. She smoothed his dark eyebrows with her thumbs before leaning in to kiss him gently on the mouth.

"Nothing is impossible, Thomas."

His sigh was full of dark memories. "For you, perhaps. Many things have been impossible for me to change."

"We don't have to be one of those things." Her certainty upon seeing Thomas at dinner was being crushed under the weight of reality, and desperation was taking its place.

She kissed him again, this time with more urgency, and grabbed hold of the collar of his jacket. His hands were warm on her back, pressing her closer. His cock lengthened and stiffened between her legs.

How many more opportunities did they have? How many shared moments remained to them? Was this to be the last one given to them? She would not squander a moment.

Victoria hiked up her night rail and fumbled with his breeches.

"Good God, woman. Are you to be the death of me?" His whisper was vehement, but he pushed her hands aside and finished the work, shoving his breeches down his thighs.

He tugged her night rail up and over her head. She gasped and dug her hands into his shoulders. She was naked while he was clothed. It took a moment to decide how she felt about the disparity. Part of her wanted to insist he disrobe, if only for her own enjoyment of his body, but she only bit her lip.

It was scandalous and naughty and offered her power when the rest of her life seemed beyond her control.

"I would have you, Thomas. One more time." She rolled her hips, sliding her slick folds over his cock. The feeling was delicious. She did it again and again until she was trembling with the pleasure.

His eyes grew hooded as he leaned his head back and watched her. He skimmed his hands over the dip of her waist and up her torso to cup her breasts and play with her nipples. The sensation made her buck harder against him. Their first time together had been as gentle as the snow falling outside the cottage. This was a tempest.

"Take my cock in hand and guide me inside you." The low rumbled of his command rolled through her like thunder.

She lifted on her knees and grasped him. He was hard and hot, and she was more than ready for him. After positioning the head of his cock at her entrance, she hesitated. Would it hurt like last time? There was only one way to find out. She lowered herself a few inches and gasped. Not from pain, but from the thrill the fullness imparted.

She craved more. Thomas slid his hands to her hips and stared at the joining of their bodies in rapt awe. Victoria wished she could see but contented herself with watching him.

She lowered herself another inch and then another. He gripped her harder, the bite of his fingers only adding to the rawness of the moment. A breathy moan slipped out of her. There was no pain, only pleasure. Bliss. Satisfaction.

Finally, she was seated against him, his cock buried deep inside of her. Waves of sensation engulfed her. She was hanging on the edge of her climax. Her body urged her to move as Thomas had done that morning.

She lifted herself, the muscles of her legs quivering, and lowered herself. It only took a dozen strokes for pleasure to consume her. She continued to move against him but clumsily. Her nipples pebbled, and he leaned in to capture one in his mouth, tugging and nipping at the sensitive peak.

He rose with her still impaled on his cock and shuffled to the bed, dropping her on the edge of the mattress. She was on her back with her legs wrapped loosely around his hips. He thrust, his rhythm fast and hard. Another wave of pleasure rose and spun her before the first had receded.

As he had their first time, he withdrew and spent on her belly, his teeth bared and his groan muffled. The heat in his gaze as it traveled over her naked body spurred her heart into a gallop.

"You are a temptress. Last time was an error in judgment. This was utter madness."

Victoria propped herself on her elbows and pushed him from between her legs with a well-placed foot in his sternum. "Why must you ruin the moment by calling our intimacies an error in judgment and madness?"

Thomas repaired his clothing, but Victoria only rose to wipe his spend from her body, then turned on him with her hands on her hips. He swallowed and held out her night rail. She ignored the offering.

"If I could—"

She held up a hand, silencing him. "If you can't—or won't—then I do not wish to discuss the future."

The lack of a future was more apt. She snatched the night rail from his hand and turned her back on him. She didn't let her tears fall until the door snicked shut.

CHAPTER 9

*G*arrick berated himself the entire trip to the Barclays' manor house and continued the self-flagellation during his reconnoiter around the grounds as evening approached. His conclusion was that it would have taken a strength he did not possess to deny Victoria when she was naked and writhing on his cock. He was as weak as a sheared Samson where Victoria was concerned.

Bloody hell, now that her natural sensuality had been unleashed, she could crook her finger and have the nearest duke on his knees between her legs. Was there a duke in attendance?

Garrick might have to introduce the gentleman to his fists. He ran a hand through his hair and jammed his hat back into place. He had to quit thinking about Victoria as his. She wasn't and never would be.

Her parting accusatory words haunted him though. Was he being noble or a coward for not pressing his suit? Perhaps neither. He was being practical. If Sir Hawkins knew Garrick had taken Victoria—twice—he'd be thrown in the Thames with much haste and no regrets.

However, if the slimmest chance of claiming happiness with Victoria existed, shouldn't he make the attempt?

According to the ancient groundskeeper, the deep gulley marked the boundary, and as there was no way down or over, Garrick turned around. He exited the woods surrounding the Barclay property on the western side of the manor. He stopped in the shadows of the trees at the edge of the manicured lawn to wipe the mud off his boots.

A single horseman arrived. Based on the lines of the horse alone, the man was a gentleman. Garrick squinted when a niggling familiarity wouldn't leave him be. He stalked toward the man. Surely Berkwith wouldn't be so idiotic as to make an appearance.

Berkwith was that idiotic.

He was giving instructions to the groom and directing the footman to take his satchel inside when Garrick reached him and cleared his throat.

Berkwith spun around with a smile, examined Garrick, and determined he was not someone he needed to impress. His smile turned into a frown, and he clipped out, "Yes? What do you want?"

"I wish to speak with you." Garrick intentionally didn't grant Berkwith a "sir" or "my lord." He was no gentleman and deserved no such deference.

"I'm road weary. Another time, perhaps." Berkwith turned to the entrance, adjusting his waistcoat and smoothing his hair.

Garrick grabbed the man by the back of the collar and shook him, not enough to hurt him, but hard enough to garner his attention. "You have time for a chat with me."

Berkwith sputtered a few nonsensical words before finding his tongue. "Unhand me, sirrah."

Garrick ignored his protests and force marched him away from the goggling of the groom and footman to where they could not be overheard. "Are you in possession of an invitation to this house party, Berkwith?"

"I played a hand of whist with young Mr. Barclay last evening, and he extended an invitation. He is not arriving until the morrow, but I have his letter of introduction." Berkwith pulled a wax-sealed letter from the inside of his jacket, and Garrick let him go in disgust. "Why the devil did you accost me? I should call you out."

"Please do. I would enjoy destroying you." Garrick kept his tone cold and calm, and as he hoped, Berkwith was rattled. "I accosted you because of your actions with regard to a certain young lady."

Berkwith's complexion turned waxy, showcasing the blue-and-black bruise peeking out at his temple hairline. "I don't know what you are referring to. Who do I have the pleasure of speaking with?"

"If it's a pleasure to be speaking with me, I must be doing this wrong," Garrick said dryly. "You know exactly what I'm referring to. A young lady was attacked. You—supposedly a gentleman—retreated and left her to the mercy of the streets."

Berkwith's mouth opened and closed, but nothing emerged. His eyes were huge with fear.

"This is what is going to happen. I will allow you to remain this evening as it is late. However, you will make your excuses to the Barclays and depart in the morning." When Berkwith made a noise to argue, Garrick held up his hand, and the other man snapped his mouth shut. "In addition, if I hear a hint of scandal attached to either lady involved in your mad scheme, I will make sure your body is never found. Is that clear?"

Berkwith nodded vigorously enough to overcome the pomade on his hair.

Garrick crossed his arms on his chest and raised his chin. "You are dismissed."

Berkwith turned and made his way to the front door as if the devil's own hounds were in pursuit. Garrick allowed himself a smile, strolled around the house, and entered through the side entrance.

While he might not be a traditional servant, neither was he an invited guest. Therefore, the room he'd received along the bachelor corridor had been a surprise. It was small but plush and exceedingly comfortable.

Gaiety spilled from the drawing room where the assembled guests were gathered for merrymaking. He glanced through the door and caught sight of Victoria. She was talking with Lady Eleanor, Lord Percival, and an unknown gentleman. She wore the green gown from her fitting at the modiste. The color highlighted her pale skin and black hair. A golden ribbon weaved through her hair like a crown.

A pang reverberated in his chest as he turned to make his way to his room. Alone. He'd won his battle with loneliness long ago in the orphanage. Yet there was no mistaking the feeling. He was lonely. Not for just anyone, but for Victoria.

"Garrick." Sir Hawkins quickstepped from the drawing room to intercept him.

"Yes, sir?"

"Berkwith had the audacity to show his face at the party. Did you see him? I have a good mind to garrote him myself."

"I hope you don't plan on asking me to murder a peer." Garrick raised an eyebrow, but Sir Hawkins merely harrumphed. Garrick continued, "The situation is handled. He will be leaving in the morning."

Sir Hawkins's outrage deflated slightly. "You should have turned him out tonight."

"The man is a coward and an opportunist, but he isn't evil."

"But he knows Victoria was... He could speak indiscreetly."

"I made clear he wouldn't enjoy the consequences if a single indiscreet word falls from his lips."

"Very well then." Sir Hawkins's eyes narrowed on Garrick.

"Clean up and change into your best clothes, then meet me in the library. I wish to speak with you."

"Yes, sir."

Sir Hawkins turned on his heel and disappeared into a book-lined room. Garrick found warm water waiting in his room. After repairing his appearance, he changed into a pair of dove-gray pantaloons, a silver-and-cream-striped waistcoat, and navy frock coat. He kept his cravat knot simple and smoothed back his hair. The small looking glass reflected back a man who would never be mistaken for a gentleman, no matter how fine the wrappings.

He joined Sir Hawkins in the library. The spymaster stood at the fireplace and stared pensively into the flames. Garrick cleared his throat.

"Ah. Pour yourself a brandy if you wish, Garrick."

Garrick wasn't one to turn down fine spirits. He joined Sir Hawkins with a tumbler in hand. "What do you require of me, sir?"

"I want you there." Sir Hawkins didn't spare him a glance.

"Where?"

"In the drawing room and at dinner. I want you to keep an eye on Berkwith."

"Would you prefer that I throw him out tonight? I could have accomplished that without changing clothes."

"That won't be necessary." Sir Hawkins turned to pace along the edge of the rug with military precision, his hands linked behind his back. "There's another matter we need to discuss."

The back of Garrick's neck heated, and his collar tightened like a noose. He forced himself not to fidget. What did Sir Hawkins suspect? Part of Garrick wanted to confess his feelings. He wanted to claim Victoria for more than a night.

But even now she was socializing with gentlemen who could raise her standing in society. Was it fair of him to force her hand? He wanted her to have the power to choose her destiny, and in doing so, he must accept that he was not the wise choice.

"You have become a skilled organizer with a head for strategy. The men respect your opinion and obey your commands without question. In short, you are a fine leader, and it's time for you to actually lead. You will no longer be in my employ."

The direction of the conversation was so unexpected, Garrick could do little but gape. Was Sir Hawkins sending him to the front lines to be killed because of his indiscretion with Victoria? It was no less than he deserved. "You're sacking me?"

Sir Hawkins paused his pacing to grip the back of the armchair between them and raise a brow. "There is a position being created under the purview of the Home Office that I have recommended you for. Most would consider this a promotion. If you acquit yourself well, further opportunities will open to you."

While the position might well offer him a boost in standing, Garrick could only focus on the fact he would be officially, finally separated from Victoria. Their social circles wouldn't align, and he would never see her. It was an effective, nonlethal way of quashing any further attachment. It was exactly what he had decided for himself, yet the thought of never again seeing her traipse down the stairs with a smile for him was devastating.

His mind riffled through the implications. Sir Hawkins must be aware of the attachment in the first place. Or at least he suspected it. Garrick quaffed the remainder of the brandy in his glass and straightened his cuffs. "Thank you for the recommendation. When do I report for duty?"

"In the new year. Tonight, however, you still work for me, and I want you to keep an eye on Victoria." Sir Hawkins took a seat in the armchair and opened the book on the side table.

"You aren't joining in the merrymaking?"

"Too much noise rattles my thoughts and gives me a headache. I'll join the group for dinner."

Garrick nodded and left Sir Hawkins to his solitude, pausing outside the door to calm his own racing thoughts. He felt adrift in more ways than one. It was difficult to be grateful when he could only focus on everything he was losing.

Losing Victoria was heartbreaking, but that wouldn't be his only loss. Sir Hawkins was more than an employer, and Garrick grieved the end of their association. He was also unaccountably hurt Sir Hawkins could dismiss him so readily.

With heavy feet, he made his way to the drawing room. A game of charades was in progress. He planted himself behind a Greek-style bust of some unfortunate Barclay ancestor with a large nose and narrow-set eyes and stared at Victoria.

She was seated on a lounge next to Lady Eleanor, laughing and calling out guesses to the pantomime being performed by Mr. Barclay, their host. Victoria touched her nape and twisted around. They locked eyes, and her smile turned tremulous. The noise around him faded until it was just the two of them.

Lady Eleanor grabbed Victoria's arm and whispered something in her ear. Her gaze broke with his, and Garrick followed the direction of her attention. Lord Berkwith had arrived, looking fresher and attired in a dapper, extravagantly patterned blue-and-green waistcoat and bottle-green velvet jacket. Only the half-hidden bruise along the hairline at his temple betrayed the harrowing experience he'd muddled through by luck and cowardice.

Berkwith smiled broadly at Lady Eleanor, who rose as if he were a puppet master. Victoria made a grab for her wrist, but it was too late. Lady Eleanor drifted over to speak with Berkwith. Someone guessed that Mr. Barclay was trout fishing, and a round of clapping ensued. A young lady bounced up and chose a slip of paper from a gentleman's black hat for her turn.

Victoria rose and meandered through the room, stopping to chat with ladies and gentlemen, but Garrick could feel the ties that bound them growing shorter as she worked her way closer and closer.

"I suppose Father sent you to keep an eye on me," she murmured before taking a sip of wassail.

"Mostly due to Berkwith, but I don't expect him to cause any trouble."

She sent him a side-eyed glance. "Did you threaten him with bodily injury?"

He harrumphed. "Of course I did."

He was rewarded with a smile that was a lighthouse to his adrift soul. What would happen when he no longer had her smiles and wit to keep him from drowning in his loneliness?

"I do hope Eleanor doesn't make a fool of herself over him." Victoria shook her head and turned to regard him. "I've rarely seen you attired for company. You look exceedingly handsome."

"The sharpness of your eyesight has now been called into question, Miss Hawkins."

"It is you who fail to recognize your charms in the looking glass." Her flirty eyes kindled a fire in his chest. Their banter had taken on new dimensions now they were intimately acquainted.

He smiled. How could he not? Just as he was debating the merits of yet another bout of madness in the middle of the night, Lord Percival approached and made a bow. "Miss Hawkins, would you take a turn about the room with me?"

Lady Hawkins had stepped closer, her glare doing its best to slice him away from Victoria. What could Garrick do but cede the field? He inclined his head and retreated with a murmured, "Enjoy your evening, Miss Hawkins."

Lord Percival monopolized Victoria's attention for the rest of the evening. He even escorted her to dinner. Three long tables were arranged in the large dining room. Garrick found himself sitting in the corner next to a local curate who seemed to be practicing his Christmas sermon on the table.

Victoria was seated between Lord Percival and another gentleman Garrick didn't recognize. She favored them with smiles and laughs, and both men seemed to take equal delight in her. And why wouldn't they? She was witty, intelligent, and beautiful.

His stomach soured, and by the time the sweet pudding arrived for dessert, his appetite had been stamped out. Was he jealous? Most assuredly so. Had he any right to his jealousy? Not a whit.

With a trip to the village planned for some guests in the morning, the party broke up soon after port was taken by the men. Garrick sent Berkwith one last withering look before heading upstairs, not to his room, but to tuck himself behind a pedestal and vase in an alcove down the hall from Victoria's room. He would sleep better knowing Victoria had arrived there safely.

The sound of feminine voices drifted up the stairs, and Garrick imitated a statue. Lady Eleanor, Lady Hawkins, and Victoria strolled toward him. After exchanging "good-nights," Lady Eleanor entered her room.

Lady Hawkins stopped in front of her door. "You enjoyed Lord Percival's company this evening."

"He is charming." Victoria fiddled with her lace cuffs.

"But?"

"Just because I enjoyed our dinner conversation doesn't mean I wish to spend the rest of my life with him by my side."

"Not yet, perhaps, but it's a promising start. I'll send Margery over as soon as she tends to me." Lady Hawkins leaned in to brush a kiss in the air next to Victoria's cheek and disappeared into her room.

Victoria made her way to her door but hesitated with her hand on the latch. "Why are you lurking in the ladies' hallway?"

He grunted. How had she seen him? Was he getting careless? He stepped out and shushed her, motioning her inside her room. "I wanted to assure myself you were safely abed."

"Safely abed? Is that what you're calling it?" Her tone was dryly amused but turned dark. "I'm tired of keeping secrets, Thomas."

Didn't she realize he would stand on a mountaintop and declare his devotion to her if he could? "I understand."

"Do you?" Her eyes narrowed on him.

In that moment, what he understood was that any spark of hope had been snuffed out. He was merely a pawn to be sacrificed by Sir Hawkins. This was the end.

But if it was to be their end, he would leave with one last kiss.

He stepped forward and cupped her face, tilting her head back. The brace of candles at the entrance made her eyes dance with light and life. "I love you, Victoria. That is a secret I will no longer keep to myself."

Her breath hitched, and her lips parted, but he didn't give her a chance to respond. His lips met hers with all the longing, regret, and anger of a last kiss, and she responded in kind. It was in turns gentle and fierce.

Knowing their time was short, Garrick broke away and hugged her close, trying to memorize her scent and warmth and softness. He ran his hands down her back to map her curves so he could find his way back to her in his dreams.

Then he stepped away, leaving her swaying on her feet, lightly touching her kiss-swollen lips. They stared at one another for a long moment. He slipped out the door and retreated to the far end of the corridor to the servant's staircase. And not a second too soon.

Margery emerged from Lady Hawkins's room to rap softly

on Victoria's door. She answered and ushered the lady's maid inside. Before she disappeared, she cast a glance up and down the hallway, but this time she didn't see him in the shadows.

The shadows were where he belonged and where he would remain.

CHAPTER 10

*V*ictoria and Eleanor strolled arm in arm through the
garden on their way to gather pinecones at the line
of trees at the back of the terraced lawn. The ground was
patched with snow in the shadows and mud in the bright
sunshine.

It was the first time Victoria had been able to speak with her
friend in private since Lord Berkwith's unexpected arrival the
evening before. "Have your tender feelings toward Lord Berkwith changed since everything that happened?"

"Of course not." Eleanor barked, but her sigh softened the
knee-jerk defensiveness of her answer. "I don't know. If I had
kept the meeting with him at the Bear and the Crown, what
would have become of me? I wouldn't have had a Mister
Garrick to ride to my rescue. By your own telling, Lord Berkwith was incapable of dealing with them. He didn't even
attempt to rescue you. Wasn't that dastardly?"

"I'm nothing to Lord Berkwith. He might have put up a fight
to save you. But don't forget, the men weren't actually after you.
You and Lord Berkwith might even now be wed if I hadn't
appeared in your stead." Even as she made the declaration, the

same question niggled. How had the men known to follow her when she had only made the decision to take Eleanor's place mere hours earlier?

"I can't help but think that a true gentleman would have rescued you." Eleanor flashed Victoria an uncertain look. "Do you approve of a match with him?"

Lady Hawkins's assessment came flooding back. Eleanor did deserve better. Victoria stopped under the leafless branches of an oak and took Eleanor's hands in hers. Winter had blunted the undergrowth, but bushes reached out of the woods, seeking sunlight.

"Do you truly love him?"

"He says such pretty things to me. My mother favors Mr. March. He is rich but so old. If I were able to choose…" Eleanor tipped her head back and looked to the sky, blinking back tears. "I envy your freedom."

"Oh, Eleanor—"

A noise in the woods whipped Victoria's head around. The two men from the alley pounced before Victoria could gather the air for a scream. A kerchief was shoved into her mouth, and a gag tied around her head.

She used the heel of her hand and punched the man on the bridge of his nose.

"Ye bloody bitch." One man held her hands together behind her back while the other bound them at the wrist. Victoria craned around to see Eleanor. She had either swooned, or the men had bashed her unconscious.

She kicked at the man she had punched, aiming for his knee but only managing to hit the top of his shin. Still, it must have pained him somewhat, because he released a longer, more colorful string of curses.

"There's no one to save you, my lady." The man tossed her over his shoulder.

Her breath left her in a whoosh. Panic rose up like a fog,

obscuring everything but her need for air. Finally, she was able to pull in a deep breath through her nose. After a dozen more, she accepted she wasn't yet dying.

Branches and brambles picked at her gown. A branch whipped back from their passing and scratched her cheek. A drop of blood trickled toward her temple. Her hands were numb, and her wrists grew raw as she worked against the coarse rope.

How had these men managed to evade her father's extensive grasp in London? Even though they had captured her easily, they did not seem unusually skilled. After all, she had landed two blows. That gave her hope. As did the fact the men did not bother to hide their tracks.

At first, she tried to keep her head raised to mark their progress, but all she could see were trees. When the ache in her neck became unbearable, she counted their paces instead and estimated they'd walked at least a mile.

Twice they crossed stiles. One man passed her to the other like a sack of potatoes. Both times, she managed to inflict damage by way of a well-placed knee. Once in the stomach, and once in the chest. Neither hit their mark of the nether regions. Still, she garnered immense satisfaction at their grunts and curses of pain.

"My sister is going to teach you a lesson, my lady." The words "my lady" dripped with derision, but Victoria focused on the nugget of information offered freely.

His sister was the mastermind? That lent an air of loyalty and not greed to her abductors' motivations. The danger rose a notch. Men could be turned through avarice, but familial bonds made the proposition more difficult.

The scent of woodsmoke tickled her nose as they entered a clearing. Less than a minute later, she passed from sunshine to shadows before being dumped on a dirt floor. The sudden change in attitude dizzied her. Not to mention the wave of pain coming from her bottom and hands from landing on them. She shifted to her side, desperate to evaluate her surroundings.

She was in a hut. No, a hovel. Leaf litter piled in the corners, and the smell was musty and animal-like. A fire burned, and as much smoke filled the room as went up the crude chimney. Her eyes watered, and a cough threatened behind the gag.

A woman emerged from the corner. Victoria awkwardly maneuvered herself to sitting and blinked to bring her into focus. She wore a veiled hat very similar to the one Victoria had commissioned two years ago to hide behind during her unchaperoned jaunts. The woman pointed at Victoria and turned to her brother. "Why the devil did you bring her?"

"It's Lady Eleanor. Like you asked."

"You dolt. That's Miss Hawkins."

The man squinted at Victoria. "Nay. She's the one who met with the toff at the Bear and the Crown."

The woman paced in the small space, punching one balled fist into her other hand. Her voice. It was familiar. And just like that, everything clicked into place.

"Mrs. Leighton?" Except it sounded like she said "blah, blah, blah?"

Mrs. Leighton spun to regard her. Something in Victoria's eyes must have signaled her recognition, because the woman let out a curse that would be common on the docks and waved her hand toward her brother. "Remove her gag, John."

The woman raised the black netting of her veil. The deferential expression the milliner wore in her shop had been replaced by a zealot's madness.

Victoria's mouth was dry and sore from the gag. She daubed her tongue along her lips before saying, "You meant to take Eleanor from the start."

"Of course I did. What would I want with the likes of you?"

If her situation weren't so dire, Victoria might have laughed.

No wonder the abduction had never made sense. Once again, her father's adage about making assumptions had proved true.

"But why Eleanor?" Certainly, Lord Stanfield had money, but not outrageous sums, or else they would have taken a town house closer to the ton's stars in Mayfair.

Mrs. Leighton's lips drew into a thin line, and she didn't answer. Grooves alongside her mouth deepened, and a wrinkle appeared between her eyes. Mrs. Leighton was older than Victoria had first guessed.

What made a woman who supported herself through a successful business resort to abduction... and perhaps worse?

Love made everyone a little mad, didn't it?

Lord Berkwith had been the one to suggest using Mrs. Leighton as a go-between, and she had seen him duck into the tailor's shop next door as they arrived at the milliner shop. "You and Berkwith are lovers."

"Randall loves me." The statement hit like the bang of a fist on a table.

"That's odd, because he told me that he loves Eleanor." Victoria kept her voice cool and even.

Mrs. Leighton swallowed hard and then pointed her finger at Victoria. "Why were you at the meeting with Randall at the Bear and the Crown? Were you trying to take him for yourself?"

"Hardly. Eleanor grew leery about meeting Lord Berkwith at such a place, so I went in her stead to pass along a message." Victoria went on the offensive. "Do you expect Lord Berkwith to marry you?"

"He loves me." Desperation drowned out the earlier surety in the statement.

"He may love you, but he will marry for money. He must in order to save his lands and legacy."

"No. He will marry me."

Arguing would not convince her of Berkwith's faithlessness.

Victoria tried a new tack. "Now you know who I am, I beg you to return me to the manor house before I'm missed."

"I cannot. You will summon the authorities, and we will be hanged." Mrs. Leighton's unnatural calmness made the hairs prickle on the back of Victoria's neck.

"No, I won't. This will be our secret. I promise." Of course, it was a promise she would not keep, and based on Mrs. Leighton's narrowed eyes she knew this as well.

"I can't take the risk, Miss Hawkins. I apologize." She might have been apologizing for a lack of blue ribbon needed for adornment around the brim of a bonnet.

"Eleanor saw your brother and his comrade take me." Victoria pulled at her bonds, but she couldn't tell if she was making any progress because the numbness had spread up her forearms and was invading her shoulders.

Mrs. Leighton looked to her brother and raised a brow.

"The chit collapsed in a heap before I could even say boo. She knows nothing that would incriminate us."

Mrs. Leighton pointed to Victoria but spoke to her brother. "This is your mistake. Dispose of it."

That sounded ominous.

John wrenched Victoria up by her arms. Pain streaked across her shoulders, and she was unable to stifle a cry. "Can you loosen my bonds? My hands and arms hurt."

"Soon enough it won't matter. Nothing will." While the threat was clear, a crack in John's voice had Victoria forgetting about her discomfort and focusing on the man.

John wasn't a killer. He might be a thief and a brawler, and she could picture him committing any number of immoral acts, but murder? No, she didn't think so. Especially a woman.

The question was how to sway him. Logic or tears?

Victoria appealed one more time to Mrs. Leighton's sense of self-preservation, if not decency. "You are making a mistake. If you hurt me, my father will not rest until he discovers the truth. He will make you all pay dearly."

Mrs. Leighton stepped closer. The bloom of youth might have faded from her face, but a different kind of beauty emerged. Less refined, yet equally as arresting.

"Berkwith is my last chance. Someone like you wouldn't understand the position of a woman like me."

"You mean a widow?"

Mrs. Leighton barked a mirthless laugh. "I'm no widow. My mother was also a milliner. She worked until her fingers grew crooked and knobby. An overdose of laudanum took her. She was naught but forty. When she died, John and I were cast into the streets. I provided the only way I could."

John moved to stand in the doorway and look outside.

Mrs. Leighton gripped Victoria's chin and tilted her face toward the meager light of the fire, forcing Victoria to meet her glittering eyes. "I sold my body to so many men I lost count. Finally, I caught a man of means, and he got me off the streets. He was a good man."

"What happened to him?"

"Died. I took his name and the money he left me and started the shop."

"You're doing well for yourself. Why would you want Lord Berkwith?"

Mrs. Leighton let go of her chin, tugged a glove off, and held up her right hand. It was work roughened and red, the joints swollen. "I inherited the same curse. Some nights, the pain is so bad I can't sleep without the very medicine that killed my mother. Soon, I won't be able to work. And then what? My looks won't last. Randall is a decent sort. A bit dim, perhaps, but he doesn't hit me. He loves me. He does."

Despite her current predicament, sympathy welled up in Victoria.

Mrs. Leighton turned to her brother. "Throw her down the ravine. With any luck, they'll think it was an accident."

Any pity Victoria was feeling was quashed by the woman's cold pronouncement. John grabbed her elbow and yanked her out of the hut. She stumbled into him. He lost his balance and released her. For a blink, she didn't move. Then, like a bird sensing an open cage door, she ran.

She didn't get far. It wasn't even John who caught her, but a root hidden under an inch of snow. She pitched forward, unable to catch herself. Cold muck seeped through her dress. She couldn't get up, nor could she roll over. Her shoulders hurt. Her arms hurt. But mostly, her heart hurt. Was there no escape? Would she never see Thomas again to tell him how she felt?

John hauled her up.

She couldn't run. She couldn't fight. She had only one option left. She gathered a lungful of air. Her scream echoed around them and shredded until there was nothing left but silence. Even the birds had quieted. She drew in a gust of air to scream again and John bashed his fist against her temple.

The hit left her dazed and tottering toward a black abyss of unconsciousness.

CHAPTER 11

$\mathcal{T}$he scream scythed through him. An answering visceral pain rose from his own throat. Instead of answering her call, he closed his eyes and concentrated on estimating direction and distance to Victoria. Not far now, but was he already too late?

He ran, leaping over fallen trees and ripping through brambles with no thought to the damage incurred to his clothes or body. His overriding thought was Victoria. If she was dead... His heart lurched, and he shut his fears down. He would be unable to function if he allowed panic to dictate his actions.

Woodsmoke had him raising his nose like a hound, and he slowed. Crouching, he picked his way closer to the clearing. A once-abandoned crofter's hut was now occupied. Footprints trampled through snow and mud. This was where Victoria was being held.

Garrick had always wondered at the way anger manifested in men. Some let their anger grow hot and burn out of control. Those men entered the fray like a berserker, killing all in their path. That had never been Garrick's way. For him, fury invaded like a winter storm. It numbed him and encased him in ice.

He stepped into the clearing. A man yelled a warning toward the hut and ran forward. Garrick recognized him from the alley. This time he would offer no mercy. Garrick met the man with a fist. The man's nose bent in the wrong direction and blood spurted. Garrick pulled a knife from the holster under his jacket and shoved it into the man's belly. He fell to his knees and over onto his side, curled on the ground.

Garrick strode to the hut and slammed the flimsy door open with such force it swung on one hinge. He narrowed his eyes against the smoke and dimness. Only one woman occupied the hut, and it wasn't Victoria. She sat in a stiff-backed wooden chair, her face in profile. It took several blinks for Garrick to recognize her. How was a bloody milliner involved?

"What the devil are you about woman? Where is Miss Hawkins?"

"You're too late." The woman twisted to look him square in the eye. Desperation was more dangerous than loyalty to a cause. "She will be dead soon enough."

"Where is she?" When the woman only mashed her lips together, Garrick pulled a second knife from under his jacket, squat on his haunches, and pressed the tip under her chin. "Do not try me, woman. Tell me, and you may yet live to see another day."

Fear flickered like the firelight over her face, gone before Garrick was sure. Finally, she said, "My brother has taken her to the ravine, but you are too late."

Garrick didn't hesitate a moment longer. He ran for the woods in direction of the ravine, picking up the trail of a single man. His habit of reconnoitering new surroundings might prove the difference between Victoria's life and death.

No smaller set of prints was visible, which meant the man was likely carrying Victoria. He didn't allow himself to dwell on why. The extra burden would slow their progress, giving Garrick a chance. And a chance was all he needed.

Movement through the trees had him slowing. It was a man carrying a body over his shoulder. Victoria's glossy black curls bounced with his every step. Her hands were tied behind her back, and she squirmed a little in the man's hold, a breathy moan carrying through the trees.

Garrick let out a steadying breath. She was alive. That's all that mattered. He stalked the man as swiftly and silently as a cat. The coarse rope binding her hands was tight, and her movements became more pronounced. The man grunted and did something to her leg that caused her to rear up in pain. She drew in a breath, looking prepared to release it in another scream when their gazes clashed and held.

She held her scream at bay, instead speaking in a hoarse voice, but not to him. "Let me go and tell your sister I'm dead."

"You'd bring hell down upon us. No. This was my mistake, and I must fix it."

Garrick bared his teeth and closed the distance by another six feet. Hell was coming for the man whether he chose to do the right thing or not.

"Have you ever killed anyone?" she asked.

"I've done plenty, girl. Tossing you over a cliff won't keep me up at night." His voice didn't contain nearly the same confidence of his words. The man might be a bruiser used to navigating Seven Dials, but he wasn't a killer. Not yet, at any rate.

"My death will not be the end of this, you know."

The conversation, as bleak as it was, was masking Garrick's approach. Victoria knew this, and Garrick almost smiled. Her quick wits and bravery had never been in question.

"You don't understand," the man said mulishly.

"Then help me understand, John."

"My sister could have left me to fend for myself. She could have sold me to a sweeper. If she hadn't had me to care for, she could have found a respectable position in a house. Instead, she — Well, I'll do anything for her. Anything."

Winter sunlight filtered through the thinning trees. The edge of the ravine was ahead. Garrick clutched the knife and made his move. It took only five long strides to reach Victoria. He slammed his shoulder into the man's arm and sent him reeling to the side.

Victoria tumbled to the ground with a grunt. Garrick forced himself not to glance in her direction. If the man happened to kill Garrick, she would be next. John swung a meaty fist around. Garrick dipped to the right, but the punch caught the edge of his jaw. Pain exploded.

The man was on Garrick before he fully recovered, grappling for the knife. Garrick broke the hold John had on his wrist and stabbed upward. The point met flesh, and Garrick drove the knife deeper. John's eyes widened, and his grip loosened. He staggered backward into a tree and slid to the ground, still propped against the trunk, his legs splayed wide.

Breathing hard, Garrick watched the life leak from the man, then he shook himself free of the icy fury that held him in its grip. Victoria lay on her stomach, her hair out of its pins and in her face.

Garrick fell to his knees and helped her to sit, brushing her hair back with a shaking hand. A bruise was forming on her temple, and she was scratched and dirty, but she appeared otherwise unharmed.

"My arms. Can you cut me loose?" Her pain reverberated to him.

Garrick returned to the dead man, pulled the knife free and wiped the blood off as best he could on the dead leaves at his feet. He sawed through the rope binding her wrists. As it began to give and her arms moved, she groaned.

"Easy now. Let me help," he said softly, chafing her arms. "How are your hands?"

"I'm not sure. I can't feel them."

He peeled off her gloves and found her hands swollen and

unnaturally white. "I'm afraid this is going to be deuced uncomfortable."

He rubbed her hands between his, stimulating blood flow and offering her his warmth. She bit her bottom lip and grimaced, but didn't cry out. After several minutes of his ministrations, her hands had turned pink, and she could open and close her fingers.

"John is dead?" It was a surprise to hear a hint of grief in her voice.

Garrick glanced over his shoulder. "He is. Are you sorry I killed him?"

"I suppose a quick death is better than the spectacle of being hanged." She looked to where their hands were clasped together. "I do feel sorry for him though. Does that make me weak?"

"It makes you human. Do you reserve the same sympathy for Mrs. Leighton?"

"Did you... kill her also?"

"No. I spoke to her briefly to ascertain your whereabouts, but my guess is your father has her in custody."

"I was scared," she said so softly he almost didn't hear her.

"I was too," he admitted.

Her gaze darted up. "I didn't think anything could rattle you."

"Losing you could." He took a deep breath, wanting to say more but knowing he shouldn't. "Let's get you back to the house and into a bath."

He rose and helped Victoria to her feet. She swayed, and her face paled. Before she could slide back to the ground, Garrick wrapped an arm around her and brought her to his body.

"I'm so dizzy." Her voice was muffled against his shoulder.

"No wonder, considering you were hauled upside down over a man's shoulder like a sack of grain." He scooped her into his arms and picked his way through the trees. "That knock on your head isn't helping matters. I'll make certain you are examined by a physician."

She rested her head on his shoulder and trembled in his arms. "I was a mistake."

"Pardon?"

"A mistake. They meant to abduct Eleanor from the Bear and the Crown, not me. It was never a plot involving Father."

"Why Lady Eleanor?"

"Mrs. Leighton is in love with Lord Berkwith and thought to eliminate her competition."

"That was an extremely risky, not to mention foolish, plan."

"She was desperate. Her hands are arthritic. She won't be able to carry on as a milliner for much longer."

Garrick didn't say what he was thinking. No matter the state of her hands, Mrs. Leighton wouldn't make another bonnet.

"Will they show mercy?" she asked.

Garrick wasn't sure who "they" referred to. Sir Hawkins? The magistrate? Garrick felt none of the compassion Victoria struggled with. Mrs. Leighton had sentenced Victoria to die. "She'll get what she deserves."

The woods were growing sparser, and a dark gray tower of the house came into view. Victoria had gone limp in his arms, her head lolling on his shoulder. He shook her slightly, and she roused, her eyes heavy-lidded.

"You can't go to sleep, sweetheart."

"But I'm so tired."

"I know, but it could be dangerous." Head wounds were tricky and unpredictable. He lengthened his stride and ignored the burn in his shoulders and arms. He would carry her back to London if he must.

She touched his cheek, drawing his gaze to hers. "Am I truly your sweetheart?"

The terror and fury of the past hour had stripped away any pretense. "You're my love. My life."

She blinked slowly and smiled before slipping back into a stupor. A shot of fear quickened his steps. He cleared the trees and jogged across the lawn toward the front of the house.

A footman met him on the graveled drive. "Sir! Is that the missing lady?"

Garrick was out of breath. "Summon a physician. Bring hot water, clean cloth, and smelling salts to Miss Hawkins's room. Find her father, Sir Hawkins, and send him up."

The footman nodded and scampered off. Garrick clattered into the house. Several ladies emerged from the drawing room, Lady Eleanor included.

"Oh, Victoria!" Lady Eleanor cried before half collapsing in her mother's arms. "I must see her."

Garrick had not the time nor patience to deal with hysterical young women. He ignored the crowd and took the steps two at a time, finally reaching Victoria's room. He lay her on the bed and made a quick examination of her head. The contusion was swelling outward, which he knew from experience was a positive sign.

A wide-eyed maid hustled in with a basin of steamy water, clean white linen, and a kit with a small supply of medicines. She set it on the stand next to the bed. Garrick nodded his thanks and uncorked the smelling salts.

One pass of the vial under Victoria's nose roused her. She took his wrist and pushed the vial away, but didn't immediately release him. Her grip was reassuringly strong. "Where am I?"

"In your room at Barclay Manor. You're safe."

"I was safe the moment you found me."

Her words were like arrows shot straight into his heart. He had survived loss, and he would survive losing her, but he would walk the earth a ghost. Victoria would always have the best of him.

The door banged open, and Sir and Lady Hawkins strode

toward the bed. Garrick extricated himself and stepped aside, stoppering the smelling salts.

"My darling girl." Lady Hawkins sat on the edge of the bed and kissed Victoria's cheek.

Sir Hawkins joined Garrick. "We found the woman. What happened to the brother?"

"You'll find his body at the edge of the ravine to the west of the estate."

Sir Hawkins inhaled sharply. "We'll retrieve it. Good work."

"Taking Victoria was an error, sir. They wanted Lady Eleanor from the start."

"I gathered as much from the woman's rambling." Sir Hawkins chuffed. It wasn't a laugh but a sound full of irony. "I've always feared someone would exact revenge because of what I have done. I never imagined danger coming from a different source."

"Victoria is safe now."

Lady Hawkins was doing most of the talking, but Victoria had propped herself on the pillows and was answering in a whisper.

"She'll recover," Garrick added.

"Thanks to you, lad." Sir Hawkins clapped him on the shoulder and went to join his wife at Victoria's bedside.

Garrick had been dismissed as any servant would be. He backed toward the door. All the fear and fury of the day had drained away, leaving him bereft of any emotion. The emptiness threatened to drag him under. He'd only felt this way one other time. After his parents had died and the village shunned him. He'd survived that heartbreak. He would survive this one too.

But not without getting rip-roaring drunk.

Victoria's quiet voice stopped him with his hand on the latch of the door. "Thomas, don't go. Stay with me."

He turned around. Victoria held a hand out to him, parting Sir and Lady Hawkins, who had shifted to stare at him with very different expressions. Sir Hawkins with a contemplative purse of his lips, and Lady Hawkins with a disapproving frown. Garrick went to Victoria, taking her hand. It was still chilled. He rubbed it gently between his hands.

Victoria smiled up at him. "I want Thomas by my side."

Lady Hawkins made a scoffing sound. "I will stay with you as long as you need, darling. I'm sure Garrick has other duties to attend."

Victoria laughed, then winced, and touched her bruised temple. "You misunderstand me."

"You have had a shock and should rest while we wait on the physician to arrive. No need to speak of things you may regret." Lady Hawkins took Victoria's wrist and pulled her hand free of Garrick's hold.

"Oh, Mother," Victoria said in a voice laced with both sadness and humor.

"Victoria is in love with Garrick, Agatha," Sir Hawkins said. "And based on my observations, the feeling is mutual."

Garrick started around to face his benefactor and employer and mentor. As usual, Sir Hawkins's face gave no hint as to his thoughts or feelings on the matter. He could very well be imagining running Garrick through with a sword.

"How long have you known, sir?" Shock roughened Garrick's voice.

Sir Hawkins waved his hand about. "For years now. Of course, I recognized Victoria was besotted with you as a young girl, but it was only after her debut and none of the gentlemen sparked her interest that I realized her feelings were well and truly fixed on you."

Lady Hawkins plopped on the edge of the bed. "This is outrageous. You must send the young man away, Harold."

Sir Hawkins linked his hands behind his back and rocked slightly on his feet. "And you believe that will solve the problem?"

"Once Victoria is married to Lord Percival—"

"Never." Victoria sounded like her father, decisive and unyielding. "I love Thomas. I've loved him for as long as I can remember. I will marry him or no one. If, that is, he will have me?"

She glanced at him through her lashes, and his knees wobbled. If her parents weren't watching them—Lady Hawkins with daggers in her eyes and Sir Hawkins more thoughtfully—he would climb in bed with her, take her in his arms, and remain that way the rest of the day and night.

Instead, he lay a hand over his heart as if he could rip it out and offer it to her. "I've always wanted you. I will do anything and everything in my power to protect you."

"If you want to protect her, you should allow her to marry someone more suitable," Lady Hawkins said through clenched teeth.

Sir Hawkins's eyebrows quirked up. "I believe Garrick would be eminently suitable for Victoria."

"But the boy is an orphan with no prospects!"

Garrick finally understood. Sir Hawkins hadn't been trying to push him out, but set him up for this moment. "I am a man, not a boy, and I will be able to provide for Victoria, perhaps not as a peer might, but we will be comfortable."

"Garrick will be working directly for the Home Office starting in the new year. It is an important position, and he will be well compensated. His ascension has been no different than mine, and I was good enough for you, Agatha."

Lady Hawkins continued to ignore Garrick. "But you gained a knighthood and accolades and—"

"Stop, Mother." Victoria pushed herself to sitting and propped herself on a mound of pillows. "I will marry Thomas. My decision is final."

Lady Hawkins's mouth pinched shut, then she spun around and stalked out the door.

Sir Hawkins sighed and patted Victoria's hand. "She'll come around. I've had a bit more time—years, in fact—to come to terms with what I deemed a likely future."

"Sir, I should have formally asked for Victoria's hand and—"

"You have my blessing, of course." Sir Hawkins looked to the fire in the grate, a pained expression flashing. "Is a speedy marriage necessary?"

Victoria and Garrick exchanged a glance. Color flooded her face. Heat radiated off his neck, and he knew his cheeks were similarly red. Did they have no secrets left? He supposed this is what came from conducting a love affair under the nose of a spymaster.

"Ah, yes. I believe a special license would be wise, sir."

Sir Hawkins made a sound of agreement. "The physician will be here soon. I shall leave the two of you alone, but the door remains open. Is that understood?"

Victoria and Garrick spoke at the same time. "Yes, sir."

When they were finally alone, Garrick perched on the edge of the bed and caressed her cheek with the back of his hand. She grabbed it and pressed a kiss to his palm.

"That was the most courageous thing I've ever witnessed," he murmured.

"Getting myself abducted?" she asked quizzically.

"Standing up to your mother. For me. I'm humbled, and I'll do my best to make sure you don't regret the decision."

"The only regret I have is not declaring myself earlier."

Garrick chuckled. "If I'd had any hope of being welcomed as an acceptable suitor, I would have offered myself two years ago. The time we've wasted."

"No, not wasted. It happened just as it should have." She drew him closer and snuggled into his chest. "Now tell me about this opportunity at the Home Office."

He half reclined, propping one leg on the bed and leaving the other on the floor. He wasn't sure if that was enough to appease the laws of propriety or not, but they had already broken so many he decided it didn't matter. "Your father informed me yesterday I'm to transition into a new position. I assumed he was fobbing me off because he'd become aware of my inappropriate feelings for you."

"It seems it was just the opposite." She yawned.

"That he's known for so long…" Garrick shook his head in wonder at the twists and turns. Every life was full of hope and hardship and joy. Sometimes at the same time, and sometimes one grew out of another. He and Victoria would no doubt encounter hardships, but they would face them together. It had been a long time since he wasn't alone.

A knock on the doorjamb had Garrick bolting off the bed. A portly man with steel-gray hair and side whiskers came inside carrying a black bag. "Miss Hawkins. My name is Dr. Calhoun. I hear you've had quite an adventure."

"Yes, Doctor, but I'm feeling better."

"Let's examine you then." Dr. Calhoun glanced Garrick's direction with a raised brow.

"Uh, let me fetch Lady Hawkins, shall I?" Garrick backed out of the room without providing an answer. Lady Hawkins descended on him like a proverbial hawk before he was even two steps down the hall.

"The physician has arrived, I hear."

"Yes, my lady." Garrick stepped aside so she could pass.

She came to an abrupt stop and turned back to him. "I do not approve, but Harold tells me I must accept your union with my daughter."

"I love her. I will protect her." He didn't flinch away from the woman's eviscerating stare.

Garrick had always thought Sir and Lady Hawkins an odd match, but no longer. Underneath the gracious facade she presented to the lords and ladies she wooed was tempered metal, hard and unbreakable.

Her jaw twitched but lost its crushing intensity. "I wanted something different for Victoria than I found. I wanted her not to worry about her husband at every turn. I wanted her to marry a man unacquainted with death and danger."

Garrick's breath caught. He hadn't considered the cost to Victoria.

"But then again, I suppose she was always too opinionated and adventurous for any of the gentlemen here." Lady Hawkins disappeared into Victoria's room.

While they hadn't made peace, it seemed they'd reached a truce.

He loitered outside the door until the physician exited. "How is she?"

The man spared Garrick nothing more than a glance. "She'll have a headache and is covered in scrapes and bruises, but she's young and strong and will be right soon enough. I've advised her to keep to her bed tonight. I'm afraid she'll miss the Christmas Eve celebrations."

Garrick nodded and poked his head around the doorjamb. Victoria was sitting on the side of the bed, and Lady Hawkins was urging her back under the covers.

"I'm not a delicate flower, Mother. I won't wilt."

"The doctor ordered you to rest."

"I'm fine." Victoria spotted Garrick in the doorway and favored him with a smile that made him want to kiss her. "Tell her, Thomas. I'll sit on a chair in the corner, but there's no reason for me to miss tonight's fun. Will someone please order me a bath?"

Garrick joined Lady Hawkins. Victoria's dress was filthy and ripped, and she was still too pale for his liking. "I agree with your mother, actually. Although a bath and change of clothes is in order."

Lady Hawkins smiled at him like a coconspirator, and he

could see his estimation in her eyes rise. "I'll find the housekeeper."

Victoria flopped backward. "I can't believe you betrayed me."

Garrick stifled a smile and leaned over her, his hands braced on either side of her shoulders. "All the commotion of a party will only exacerbate the pain in your head. You've been through a trying experience today. You need to recover."

Her chin wobbled. "I don't want to be stuck in my room. Alone. I keep reliving it. What if you hadn't found me?"

Garrick should have seen through her bravado. "You won't be alone. I care not for parties and won't leave your side. Would you like visitors? Lady Eleanor, perhaps?"

"Yes, please," she said. "Thank you."

She clutched at his jacket and drew him down to her. He gave her what they both wanted—and what she needed—a kiss. Not a kiss of seduction, but a promise. He would keep her safe and protect her, but he would also give her freedom.

CHAPTER 12

*V*ictoria didn't want to admit her mother and Thomas had been right. She was drained and sore, and her head ached. The notion of lacing up her stays and getting pins stuck into her scalp to listen to subpar pianoforte playing made her shudder. After bathing and slipping on a night rail and dressing gown, she settled into a comfy armchair in front of the fire.

Eleanor entered with mincing steps and burst into tears when she saw Victoria.

Victoria rose, put an arm around her friend's shoulders, and drew her toward a second chair. "Come now. I don't look that ghastly, do I?"

"I'm so sorry this happened, and all because of me." Eleanor wailed the last word.

"It wasn't your fault. I mostly blame Mrs. Leighton, but Lord Berkwith deserves a portion of the fault. It seems as though he was stringing Mrs. Leighton along in order to continue enjoying her favors."

Eleanor pulled out a delicately embroidered handkerchief to daub at her eyes and nose. Victoria had never seen anyone cry more genteelly. Victoria cried like she did most things—with gusto. Her nose ran and turned red, and her eyes swelled.

Victoria corralled her wandering thoughts. "Where is Lord Berkwith?"

"He was called away before dawn. A sick aunt." The forlorn note in Eleanor's voice made Victoria shake her head.

"Don't tell me your feelings are still engaged? After everything he has done?"

"You told me yourself you thought he truly cared about me." Eleanor wouldn't look at her.

"Yes, but not more than he cares about himself. Or your dowry. If not for that, he wouldn't give you a second glance." Victoria's ordeal had stripped away her tact when it came to Lord Berkwith.

Eleanor gasped. "That's a terribly unkind thing to say."

"You are lovely and kind and will make some gentleman a wonderful wife. I'm just not certain Lord Berkwith deserves you."

Eleanor rose and fiddled with the handkerchief. She was dressed in a ruby red dress that highlighted her creamy complexion and golden-brown hair. "I'm very much afraid that I love him."

Victoria's headache grew worse with the pronouncement. She rose and stilled Eleanor's hands with her own. "After all I have endured, will you grant me a boon?"

Eleanor clutched at Victoria, the tears glimmering in her eyes only enhancing the blue. "Anything that's in my power."

"Give London one more season. If at the end you are still in love with Berkwith—and he with you—then you'll have my blessing." Victoria was counting on Lord Berkwith hying off with an easier mark before then. Better Eleanor suffer a broken heart than a lifetime stuck with a charming bounder.

Eleanor's reluctance was written plainly on her face. "I

suppose a few months won't make a difference, will they? It will give Lord Berkwith more time to win over my parents."

"Exactly." A soft rap sounded on the door. "Come in."

Thomas stepped through the door and left it ajar.

Eleanor inclined her head. "Mr. Garrick. Thank you for rescuing my dear friend."

Thomas's eyebrows quirked up, but his face remained impassive and intimidating. He didn't reply.

Before he could say something even less tactful than what Eleanor had already heard, Victoria led her toward the door. "Go have fun. It's yuletide, and you're missing all the games and food. You should see if Lord Percival requires a partner."

Laughter and the off-key tinkle of piano keys drifted up the stairs. Eleanor glanced over her shoulder at Thomas, then leaned closer to whisper in Victoria's ear, "Will you be all right with him?"

Victoria cut her smile short because it hurt her swollen temple, so she nodded. "Perhaps he is the one who should worry. I might take wild advantage of him."

Eleanor laughed, the tears and angst erased as easily as a sponge on slate. "Your jests never fail to amuse me."

Once Eleanor was out of sight down the hallway, Victoria closed the door and locked it.

"What are you doing, you minx?" Thomas crossed his arms over his chest, his mouth set in a scowl.

At first glance, he was an intimidating, scary brute. It's what made him excel at his profession. Victoria knew the truth. A shiver ran through her. That scowly mouth could do unspeakably tender things, and so could his big, hard body.

"I'm going to kiss you." Stalking him, she forced his retreat until the back of his legs hit the chair, and he plopped down. She draped herself over his lap, twined her arms around his neck, and fulfilled her promise.

She was the aggressor, plundering his mouth and wanting to

tempt him into another indiscretion. He resisted, gentling the kiss until he was sipping on her lips like a butterfly. "I shan't take you tonight."

"But I need you, Thomas." The plaintive note in her voice betrayed her frayed nerves over the events of the day. "If things had gone differently…"

He tucked her head into the warm space between his neck and shoulder. "I will not take you, but I will watch over you so you can get the rest you need."

She took a deep, shuddery breath. His scent was a familiar comfort. And it would be hers to savor forever. He was hers forever. The reality had yet to sink in.

"We will marry?" she whispered.

"With haste."

"But you did not plant your seed inside me."

His chest rumbled with what she took for a laugh. "According to my comrades, it is not a foolproof method to prevent a babe. Even so, we've waited long enough, haven't we? Unless you would like a formal wedding this spring in London?"

He shifted to see her face, but she only snuggled closer. "Not at all. The sooner I have you in my bed, the better."

This time his laugh was unmistakable. She hoped to make him laugh every day. Or at least every other day. "You did take my virtue in a most unladylike manner."

She smiled and pressed a kiss against his warm skin, her eyes falling shut as exhaustion crept over her. Her body and mind understood she was safe in his arms, and she was able to relax. "I must make an honest man of you."

"Indeed. An honest man who loves you beyond measure." A hitch in his breath had her attention. "My new position will come with dangers, Victoria. Are you sure you'd not prefer to escape the game your father and I are forced to play?"

She tightened her hold on him. "Who then would protect you?"

He hummed and brushed his lips against her aggrieved temple. Feeling his complete capitulation, she drifted into a light sleep, dimly aware when he tucked her into the bed.

"I'll keep watch over you, love," he whispered when she stirred.

She smiled and succumbed to the rest her body craved, knowing when she awoke he would be there—and they would face the future together.

The End

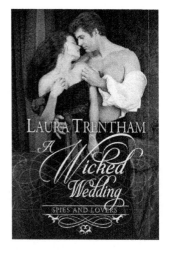

I hope you loved Thomas and Victoria! My first virgin hero! I have a Christmas novella in the series, I hope you will enjoy. A WICKED WEDDING is set after An Indecent Invitation in the timeline. In fact, if you've read An Indecent Invitation you might recall Lord Abbott cornering Gray Masterson about suspicious lights along the cliff near his country estate. Gray was too distracted by Lily at the time, but he didn't forget and makes an appearance in A WICKED WEDDING. But the story belongs to Diana and Cole, childhood friends who are drawn closer by the intrigue afoot!

Introducing the Fieldstones Adventures by Leah Trent
Interested in something hotter? And, I mean *a lot* hotter...

Call the fire department hot. Your ereader will spontaneously combust hot.

Centered on the private club introduced in An Indecent Invitation, this series highlights the ladies and gentleman who explore their deepest fantasies at Fieldstones. This is a series of *erotic* romance novellas.

Warning: Don't venture into the Fieldstones world unless you are ready and willing!

Fieldstones Adventure Novellas by Leah Trent
    An Impetuous Interlude, Fieldstones Adventure Book 1
    A Naughty Notion, Fieldstones Adventure Book 2
    A Mysterious Masquerade, Fieldstones Adventure Book 3
    A Dangerous Desire, Fieldstones Adventure Book 4
    The Fieldstones Adventures Boxset

Are you interested in receiving a FREE book?!

Join my newsletter! There will be links in your Welcome Email for TWO free books!

Sign up for Laura's Newsletter

ALSO BY LAURA TRENTHAM

*H*istorical Romance
Spies and Lovers
An Indecent Invitation Book 1
A Brazen Bargain, Book 2
A Reckless Redemption, Book 3
A Sinful Surrender, Book 4
A Wicked Wedding, Book 5
A Daring Deception, Book 6
A Scandalous Secret, Book 7
Spies and Lovers Boxset

CONTEMPORARY ROMANCE
Sweet Home Alabama Novels
Slow and Steady Rush, Book 1
Caught Up in the Touch, Book 2
Melting Into You, Book 3
Christmas in the Cop Car, Novella 3.5
The Sweet Home Alabama Collection

· · ·

HIGHLAND, Georgia Novels
A Highlander Walks Into a Bar, Book 1
A Highlander in a Pickup, Book 2
A Highlander is Coming to Town, Book 3

HEART OF A HERO Novels
The Military Wife
An Everyday Hero

COTTONBLOOM NOVELS
Kiss Me That Way, Book 1
Then He Kissed Me, Book 2
Till I Kissed You, Book 3

CHRISTMAS IN THE COP CAR, Novella 3.5
Light Up the Night, Novella 3.75

LEAVE THE NIGHT ON, Book 4
When the Stars Come Out, Book 5
Set the Night on Fire, Book 6

FIELDSTONES ADVENTURE NOVELLAS by Leah Trent
An Impetuous Interlude, Fieldstones Adventure Book 1
A Naughty Notion, Fieldstones Adventure Book 2
A Mysterious Masquerade, Fieldstones Adventure Book 3
A Dangerous Desire, Fieldstones Adventure Book 4
The Fieldstones Adventures Boxset

I love to hear from readers! Come find me:

Laura@LauraTrentham.com
www.LauraTrentham.com
Sign up for Laura's Newsletter
Join Laura's Facebook Squad

Are you interested in receiving a FREE book?!

Join my newsletter! There will be links in your Welcome Email for TWO free books!

Sign up for Laura's Newsletter

ABOUT THE AUTHOR

I hope you enjoyed *A Sinful Surrender*! If you have a chance please leave a quick review! Although, many readers know me from my Southern-set contemporary romances, the first books I wrote were the Spies and Lovers series! I grew up reading the historical "bodice rippers" of the late eighties and early nineties along with wonderful gothic romances. Now that I have the opportunity to publish all of the Spies and Lovers series, I'm so excited! The Spies and Lovers world will be expanding soon with a new series called, Laws of Attraction!

I was born and raised in a small town in Northwest Tennessee. Although, I loved English and reading in high school, I was convinced an English degree equated to starvation! So, I chose the next most logical major - Chemical Engineering- and worked in a hard hat and steel toed boots for several years. Now I live in South Carolina with my husband and two children. In between school and homework and soccer practices, I love to get lost in another world, whether it's Regency England or small town Alabama.

My first two Falcon Football books received TOP PICKS from RT Book Reviews and a STARRED review from Library Journal. KISS ME THAT WAY, Cottonbloom Book 1, won the Stiletto Contest for Best Long Contemporary and finaled in the National Readers Choice Award. THEN HE KISSED ME, Cottonbloom Book 2, was named an Amazon Best Romance of 2016 and was a finalist for the National Excellence for Romance Fiction. TILL I KISSED YOU, Cottonbloom Book 3, is a finalist in the Maggie contest. LEAVE THE NIGHT ON, the latest Cottonbloom book, was named an iBooks Best Book of the Month and a Recommended Read from NPR. AN INDECENT INVITATION and A BRAZEN BARGAIN were both finalists for the 2014 Golden Heart® Award.

I love to hear from readers! Come find me:
Laura@LauraTrentham.com
www.LauraTrentham.com
Sign up for Laura's Newsletter
Join Laura's Facebook Squad

Printed in Great Britain
by Amazon